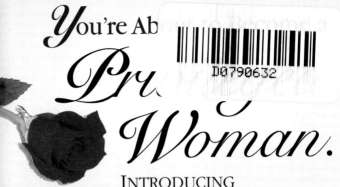

You're Ab... *to Become a*
Pr...
Woman.

INTRODUCING
PAGES & PRIVILEGES™.

It's our way of thanking you for buying
our books at your favorite retail store.

GET ALL THIS FREE

WITH JUST ONE PROOF OF PURCHASE:

◆ Hotel Discounts up to 60% at home and abroad

◆ Travel Service - Guaranteed lowest published
  airfares plus 5% cash back on tickets

◆ $25 Travel Voucher

◆ Sensuous Petite Parfumerie collection ($50 value)

◆ Insider Tips Letter with sneak previews of
  upcoming books

◆ Mystery Gift (if you enroll before 6/15/95)

You'll get a FREE personal card, too.
It's your passport to all these benefits— and to
even more great gifts & benefits to come!

There's no club to join. No purchase commitment. No obligation.

As a *Privileged Woman,* you'll be entitled to all these *Free Benefits.* And *Free Gifts,* too.

To thank you for buying our books, we've designed an exclusive FREE program called *PAGES & PRIVILEGES™.* You can enroll with just one Proof of Purchase, and get the kind of luxuries that, until now, you could only read about.

*B*IG HOTEL DISCOUNTS

A privileged woman stays in the finest hotels. And so can you—at up to 60% off! Imagine standing in a hotel check-in line and watching as the guest in front of you pays $150 for the same room that's only costing you $60. Your *Pages & Privileges* discounts are good at Sheraton, Marriott, Best Western, Hyatt and thousands of other fine hotels all over the U.S., Canada and Europe.

*F*REE DISCOUNT TRAVEL SERVICE

A privileged woman is always jetting to romantic places. When <u>you</u> fly, just make one phone call for the lowest published airfare at time of booking—<u>or double the difference back</u>! PLUS—

you'll get a $25 voucher to use the first time you book a flight AND <u>5% cash back on every ticket you buy thereafter through the travel service</u>!

FREE GIFTS!

A privileged woman is always getting wonderful gifts.
Luxuriate in rich fragrances that will stir your senses (and his). This gift-boxed assortment of fine perfumes includes three popular scents, each in a beautiful designer bottle. Truly Lace...This luxurious fragrance unveils your sensuous side. L'Effleur...discover the romance of the Victorian era with this soft floral. Muguet des bois...a single note floral of singular beauty. This $50 value is yours—FREE when you enroll in *Pages & Privileges*! And it's just the beginning of the gifts and benefits that will be coming your way!

$50 VALUE

FREE INSIDER TIPS LETTER

A privileged woman is always informed. And you'll be, too, with our free letter full of fascinating information and sneak previews of upcoming books.

MORE GREAT GIFTS & BENEFITS TO COME

A privileged woman always has a lot to look forward to.
And so will you. You get all these wonderful FREE gifts and benefits now with only one purchase...and there are no additional purchases required. However, each additional retail purchase of Harlequin and Silhouette books brings you a step closer to even more great FREE benefits like half-price movie tickets...and even more FREE gifts like these beautiful fragrance gift baskets:

L'Effleur ...This basketful of romance lets you discover L'Effleur from head to toe, heart to home.

Truly Lace ...A basket spun with the sensuous luxuries of Truly Lace, including Dusting Powder in a reusable satin and lace covered box.

ENROLL NOW!

Complete the Enrollment Form on the back of this card and become a Privileged Woman today!

Enroll Today in *PAGES & PRIVILEGES*™, the program that gives you Great Gifts and Benefits with just one purchase!

Enrollment Form

☐ *Yes!* I WANT TO BE A *PRIVILEGED WOMAN.*

Enclosed is one *PAGES & PRIVILEGES*™ Proof of Purchase from any Harlequin or Silhouette book currently for sale in stores (Proofs of Purchase are found on the back pages of books) and the store cash register receipt. Please enroll me in *PAGES & PRIVILEGES*™. Send my Welcome Kit and FREE Gifts -- and activate my FREE benefits -- immediately.

NAME (please print)

ADDRESS   APT. NO

CITY   STATE   ZIP/POSTAL CODE

PROOF OF PURCHASE

Please allow 6-8 weeks for delivery. Quantities are limited. We reserve the right to substitute items. Enroll before October 31, 1995 and receive one full year of benefits.

NO CLUB!
NO COMMITMENT!
Just one purchase brings you great Free Gifts and Benefits!
(See inside for details.)

Name of store where this book was purchased_____

Date of purchase_____

Type of store:

☐ Bookstore   ☐ Supermarket   ☐ Drugstore

☐ Dept. or discount store (e.g. K-Mart or Walmart)

☐ Other (specify)_____

Which Harlequin or Silhouette series do you usually read?

_____

Complete and mail with one Proof of Purchase and store receipt to:

U.S.: *PAGES & PRIVILEGES*™, P.O. Box 1960, Danbury, CT 06813-1960

Canada: *PAGES & PRIVILEGES*™, 49-6A The Donway West, P.O. 813, North York, ON M3C 2E8   PRINTED IN U.S.A

Alex Wished He Could Go Back
To The Teenager He'd Been...

shuffling home with Genie's voice repeating, "What a nerd," over and over again in his mind.

If he could go back, he would pat himself on the shoulder and tell himself not to worry or agonize over Genie's rejection.

He'd tell the young Alex that she would take back her words. That she would let him—no, make that *beg* him to—do all the things he'd fantasized about doing to her in his youthful dreams.

As well as a few things he'd learned later.

Dear Reader,

As always, I am proud to be bringing you the very best that romance has to offer—starting with an absolutely wonderful *Man of the Month* from Annette Broadrick called *Mysterious Mountain Man*. A book from Annette is always a real treat, and I know this story—her fortieth for Silhouette—will satisfy her fans and gain her new ones!

As readers, you've told me that you *love* miniseries, and you'll find some of the best series right here at Silhouette Desire. This month we have *The Cop and the Chorus Girl*, the second book in Nancy Martin's delightful *Opposites Attract* series, and *Dream Wedding*, the next book in Pamela Macaluso's *Just Married* series.

For those who like a touch of the supernatural, look for Linda Turner's *Heaven Can't Wait*. Lass Small's many fans will be excited about her latest, *Impulse*. And Kelly Jamison brings us a tender tale about a woman who returns to her hometown to confront her child's father in *Forsaken Father*.

Don't miss any of these great love stories!

Lucia Macro,
Senior Editor

Please address questions and book requests to:
Silhouette Reader Service
U.S.: 3010 Walden Ave., P.O. Box 1325, Buffalo, NY 14269
Canadian: P.O. Box 609, Fort Erie, Ont. L2A 5X3

PAMELA MACALUSO
DREAM WEDDING

SILHOUETTE *Desire*®
Published by Silhouette Books
America's Publisher of Contemporary Romance

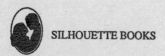

SILHOUETTE BOOKS

ISBN 0-373-05928-0

DREAM WEDDING

Printed in U.S.A.

Books by Pamela Macaluso

Silhouette Desire

*Hometown Wedding #897
*Dream Wedding #928

*Just Married

PAMELA MACALUSO

wanted to be a writer from the moment she realized people actually wrote the wonderful stories that were read to her. Since she is extremely curious and has an overactive imagination, writing is the perfect career for her. Curiosity is a necessary part of "research," and flights of fantasy can be called "plotting"—terms she prefers to "nosy" and "woolgathering."

While she loves movies, Pamela would choose a good book over any other form of entertainment. It sometimes takes a search party to get her out of a library or bookstore.

For Julie Barnes Ballinger—
Thank you for being my maid of honor,
my sister
and, most importantly,
my friend.

One

"Miss Hill! Miss Hill! The Terminator has Joey!"

Genie Hill turned to the breathless, wide-eyed boy who had burst through the school office door. She reached out her arm to take hold of his shoulder before the sheer momentum of the running fourth grader could carry him past her.

"Slow down, Paul." The child's pent-up energy transferred into up and down motion in front of his teacher. "Now, tell me again. Where's Joey?"

"The Terminator has him."

She'd heard him right the first time. Genie was sure the futuristic cyborg from the series of Terminator movies was not likely to be in Wiley, Georgia, but the fear in Paul's eyes frightened her. "Has him where?"

"Out front by the bike rack."

At least they were close by—*if* they were still there. Life was usually quiet in the small, sleepy town. There had never been a case of child abduction, but...

Her heartbeat accelerated as she turned and headed quickly for the door.

Paul started to follow.

"You stay here," Genie told him.

"Should I call Sheriff Conroy?" Annabelle Foster, the office secretary, called after her.

"If I'm not back in three minutes."

Genie ran the last few steps, jerked open the door and dashed out. Her gaze flew to the bike racks. She didn't see Joey, but she saw the back of a tall, blond man, dressed in blue jeans and black leather jacket. He was looking down at something in front of him.

A few more swift steps and she saw Joey, staring up, his eyes as wide open as his mouth usually was and his lips pressed tightly closed.

Without slowing, she moved until she stood directly in front of her student. Looking up, she realized her action had put her much closer to the tall stranger than she cared to be.

His hostile gaze, which had been aimed at the nine-year-old, now fastened on the rise and fall of the feminine curves beneath her burgundy sweater. His scowl turned into a smooth smile, and his gaze flicked downward to the black loafers on her feet. When it slowly moved up to meet hers, her already racing heart sped up even more.

"Well, well . . . what do we have here?"

A deep, warm voice, with no trace of a southern accent. Gorgeous blue eyes, a strong chiseled jawline, a sexy smile with a dimple on the right cheek . . .

Joey clutched at Genie's hand and peeked around her side, breaking the trance she'd been falling into. She turned back into a teacher concerned for her pupil. "That's what I'd like to know. What do we have here?" She was glad her uneasiness didn't show in her voice.

"Maybe you should ask the little guy."

She tilted her chin up, refusing to be intimidated. "Whatever he did doesn't give you the right to accost and scare him."

"I didn't accost him, angel. I was just trying to find out who he was so I could make arrangements to talk to his parents."

"What did Joey do?"

"Joey? Is that your name, sport?"

Genie looked at Joey.

He looked back. "I didn't say a word to him, Miss Hill, just like you taught us."

She reached down and ruffled his red hair.

"Since he's got the never-talk-to-strangers routine down, maybe you should work on teaching him not to bully other kids."

Joey smiled, managing to look completely innocent.

Genie turned to the stranger, coming face-to-face with his broad chest. An uneasy feeling crept over her.

Moving her gaze down, she noticed several patches of wetness on his black T-shirt and a small piece of red balloon clinging to the stretchy fabric.

Oh, my!

As she watched, he moved one long-fingered, masculine hand to brush off the balloon.

Fascinated by the beauty of his male muscles, she was unable to keep her gaze from dropping farther down. The wetness stopped above the blue jeans.

Thank heavens!

As it was, the tight-fitting denim had her quickly dropping her gaze to check out the black leather motorcycle boots—if the *jeans* had been wet . . .

"See anything you like, angel?"

Genie felt her cheeks grow warm. Ignoring his question she asked, "I take it Joey threw the water balloon?"

"He was aiming at the other little guy. The one who ran into the building."

Paul hadn't been wet. Joey must have missed him. Too bad he hadn't missed this guy, also. She looked at Joey. "I think you should apologize."

Joey hung his head. "I was aiming for Paul, and I'm sorry the water balloon hit you, sir."

"I hope you'll think twice before bullying someone else again."

"Yes, sir."

The angry look on the man's face showed no sign of softening. Joey's apology was contrite and sincere. He'd even remembered to end with sir. Genie thought the man could at least stop scowling. Or have the courtesy not to look so attractive while doing it.

"Why don't you go on into the office, Joey? I'll be along in a few minutes," Genie told him. With Joey safely on his way, she could step away, but didn't want to give the impression that she was backing down. "Throwing water balloons doesn't make a child a bully."

The man gave a short bitter laugh. "What would you call it, then?"

"It depends on the situation. My guess is that the balloon was payback for the rubber spider in Joey's lunch box today."

A police siren started up on the other side of the town square. Although the fastest route from the sheriff's office to the elementary school would have been on foot, Genie suspected Sheriff Conroy was heading their way. She should have told Joey to tell Annabelle everything was all right.

"Let me get this straight," the stranger continued. "If you're doing something as retaliation, you're exempt from being considered a bully?"

"You're making a generalization. I'm talking about a specific case."

He ran his hand through his hair. "What criteria would you use to define a bully?"

"A bully pulls malicious pranks."

"You don't think throwing water balloons at an unsuspecting victim is malicious? Maybe you should ask Joey's intended target how he feels."

"Water balloons could be used for malicious pranks, but I'm sure in this case it was more of a practical joke. These two are the best of friends—"

"With friends like that, who needs enemies?"

The siren grew louder until it cut off in mid-wail behind her. Genie turned.

Sheriff Zeke Conroy stepped out of his cruiser. He looked the stranger up and down, adjusted his holster and walked toward them. Zeke had been sheriff for the last twenty years. The only other job Genie could imagine him doing would be as an actor who specialized in portraying small-Southern-town sheriffs.

Grateful for an excuse to put some space between herself and the too-handsome stranger, Genie stepped back to make room for the new arrival.

"Trouble, Eugenia?"

"Just a misunderstanding, Sheriff," the blond man said.

Zeke's eyes narrowed slightly. "You got any ID?"

The man crossed his arms over his chest and looked at Zeke. "Of course."

"Mind if I take a look at it, son?"

The stranger reached into his back pocket, pulling the denim of his fly even tighter. Genie turned her attention to the building behind him where Annabelle, Joey, Paul and an assortment of other folks had gathered to watch.

"New York City. You just passin' through, then?" Zeke's tone clearly implied that the answer had better be yes.

Genie had noticed the man didn't have a southern accent, but it wasn't a New York accent, either.

"I'll be here a week."

"Our campground is closed for the season and the closest motel is over in Calhoun."

"I'm staying with family."

"Family, huh? Now, just who would that be Mr., er..." He looked at the card in his hand, which Genie assumed was a driver's license. "Mr. Alexander Lee Dalton. You one of Grandee's kin?"

Alexander Dalton?

The name was familiar to Genie, but the only picture that came to mind was of a skinny, nerdy kid with horn-rimmed glasses and bad skin.

That Alex Dalton had come to Wiley every year for summer vacation and stayed with Grandee. He'd never fit in with the rest of the kids. The only personal contact she'd had with him had been when her mother had hired him to tutor her the summer she'd repeated algebra.

There was nothing in this gorgeous specimen of maleness to link him to the boy she remembered. Of course with the size of the Dalton clan and the way they'd trickled off to live in other places, it was possible there was more than one Alex Dalton.

"Yes, she's my great-grandmother," Alex told Zeke.

"You here for her birthday celebration?"

"That's right."

"One hundred years." He handed Alex his license. "We should all be so lucky." He turned to Genie.

"Well, Eugenia, what is it that Alex here did to make you call for help?"

She didn't like the way his smile had changed and was sure any answer she gave him would be just a formality. "Paul came running into the office saying that a...a stranger had Joey. I had Annabelle call you since I wasn't sure what we were dealing with." She'd gone out looking for the Terminator and instead found another capital-T word—Trouble.

Zeke shrugged. "You satisfied now that everything is okay? After all, a kin to Grandee can't be a stranger."

"The children don't know him, and he scared them half to death by stopping Joey." He'd also scared her half to death! Besides, wasn't there a law somewhere forbidding a man from looking so good in blue jeans?

"Just a misunderstanding. Right, Alex?" Zeke reached out and shook his hand. "Enjoy your stay with us."

He returned the sheriff's handshake. "I intend to." As Zeke turned away, Alex looked at Genie. "You're sorry he didn't throw the book at me, aren't you?"

Her hands tightened into fists. "Maybe if he'd cuffed you and hauled you off to spend a few hours in the Wiley jail, you'd think twice about approaching unaccompanied children."

"You'd like to see me in handcuffs? Maybe Sheriff Conroy has a spare pair he'll loan us. I'm game if you are."

Genie was speechless.

Alex chuckled, then flashed her another of his sexy smiles. "See you around, Genie."

Genie?

How did he know friends called her Genie? Zeke had called her Eugenia, and Joey had called her Miss Hill. Had he made a lucky guess at her nickname or could he be the same Alex who had tutored her?

Genie watched him walk down the sidewalk. Concern for Joey had been her main focus when she'd come out. With the youngster safe, she was free to notice that Alex Dalton's jeans fit as nicely across the back as they did across the front.

This couldn't be the same guy....

She watched until he reached a large black and chrome motorcycle, then she turned toward the office.

Paul and Joey dashed down the steps. "Miss Hill, what did the Terminator say to you?"

Joey snorted. "Grow up, Paul. The Terminator is just a character in a movie. He's not real. It's an actor. Arnold Schwarzkopf."

"Schwarzkopf's that Desert Storm guy, you idiot!"

"Well, it's Arnold Schwarts-something," Joey fired back, then looked at Genie. "Is Arnold still mad that I hit him with the balloon, Miss Hill?"

"Sorry to disappoint you two, but it wasn't Arnold Schwarzenegger. The man's name is Alexander Dalton, and he's one of Grandee's great-grandsons. He wasn't happy about getting hit with a water balloon,

but the reason he stopped you was that he was concerned you might be bullying Paul.''

The boys exchanged puzzled glances.

"Can we go home now?" Paul asked.

"Sure. See you tomorrow, guys."

After a quick wave goodbye, the two friends took
off. Genie chuckled as she watched them. She could see
that from their height Alex might look like Arnold
Schwarzenegger.

From what she'd seen, he had a terrific build. Probably not the bulk of a weight lifter... or a professional
football player. The thought entered her mind before
she could squelch it.

She shouldn't be surprised, though. Even now, any
number of things could set off memories of Will
Tucker. Today she guessed it was the thoughts of high
school algebra that had her thinking of her ex-fiancé's
profession. After all, they'd been high school sweethearts.

Genie turned and walked toward the office to finish
checking out for the day. She didn't want to think
about Will Tucker.

Even more, she didn't want to think about Alex
Dalton, his sexy smile or the peculiar awareness he'd
stirred in her.

"So, Genie Hill didn't marry Will Tucker?" Alex
asked his great-grandmother.

Grandee shook her head as she rinsed off the glass
she was holding and handed it to Alex for drying.

"Nope. They called it off a month before the wedding."

He was surprised. Genie and Will had been "the couple" the last few summers his parents had shipped him off to Georgia for vacation.

Since Joey had called her *Miss* Hill, she must not have married anyone else, either.

He put the glass in the cupboard. Grandee had a dishwasher but rarely used it, saying she liked to end her day of chores with the familiar feel of warm soapy dishwater. Here in her house, her word was law. If she said the dinner dishes were going to be washed by hand, by golly the dinner dishes were washed by hand.

Born a week short of one hundred years ago as Sarah Mary Thomas, Grandee had married and become Sarah Dalton. Her first grandchild called her Grandma Dalton, then shortened it to Grandma D. Over time it had evolved into Grandee and now it was the only name she went by.

Alex reached out and took the next glass from her. "Does Genie teach at the elementary school?"

"Yes, dear. Fourth grade, I think. Your cousin Donny's boy has her. I think he's in the fourth grade. I can't keep track of the young 'uns the way I used to. I've got the grandchildren and the great-grandchildren down, but these great-great-grands..."

Genie had ended up becoming a teacher. Alex wondered what had made her choose that over the glamorous life Will's football career could have provided her. Or maybe Will had been the one to break it off.

He wanted to know more, but Grandee was a sharp one and would catch on if he kept asking about Genie. "How is cousin Donny?"

Grandee set off on a roll, filling him in on all the relatives, including a listing of who was coming to her birthday party. Alex listened, but found Genie crossing his mind frequently.

Genie Hill had been a real looker in high school. Dark brown hair that glimmered in the sun, light hazel eyes that sparkled when she smiled.

Not that her smile had ever been directed at him back then.

He'd expected her to grow into a beautiful woman, rather than the ordinary-looking one who'd come racing to the rescue of that little prankster. Her hair, which had once swung enticingly around her shoulders, was now tucked into a tight bun, which did nothing for her.

She did have a point, though. Approaching the child hadn't been wise. But being christened with a water balloon had struck a chord within him.

He'd lost count of the times Will Tucker and his cronies had been lying in wait for him when he'd ventured away from the safety of Grandee's. Whether he was going to the grocery store, movie theater or the library, he always seemed to end up wet, either coming or going.

And the balloons weren't the worst of it—*Four-eyes, Einstein, Specs, Crater-face*—that name-calling hurt more than the water.

The last few summers had been more peaceful. Will was occupied with Genie and spent less time picking on his regular targets.

Genie.

Alex had had a major crush on her. Living for the school vacation, praying that this summer she would notice him.

He was fairly certain she hadn't recognized him today. He would admit he'd changed a lot since she'd seen him last. Changed as much as she had. Only difference was that his changes had been for the better.

Time had made some of them, working out and a more active life-style had helped. Contact lenses had banished the horn-rims most of the time, although he had a pair of wire-frame glasses he wore occasionally.

But the biggest changes were the ones within.

He'd been a loner most of his life. Not by choice. He'd tried to fit in with other children, both at home in California and here in Wiley where he'd spent his summers. He hadn't been successful in either place. In fact he hadn't had any real friends until he'd met Rorke O'Neil and Jesse Tyler while he'd been working on his MBA at MIT.

The three of them had hit it off right away. Both Rorke and Jesse had successful relationships with women—more than their fair share, as far as he'd been concerned. He'd said as much, and they'd taken him under their wing and taught him the ropes.

The first thing Rorke had told him was to lose the pocket protector and the horn-rims. Then he gave him some pointers on how to talk to women.

Talk them right out of their silk and lace and into his sheets. Once he had them there, fortunately, Mother Nature had taken over.

Now he had his pick of women. He was certain he could have Miss Eugenia Hill, too. If he wanted her.

He thought back to the moment her burgundy sweater had come into his view. It had been on the baggy side, like the dark gray skirt she wore with it. But with her breathing deeply from her sprint, he'd seen enough to suspect somewhere underneath all that material she was hiding a nicely developed feminine body.

The grown-up version of the body that had tormented his adolescent fantasies, back when she'd paraded around in short shorts and halter tops.

He couldn't have had her then, but he could have her now.

Thinking of her sour expression, severe hairstyle and sensible shoes put a damper on his enthusiasm. Yet the idea of Genie wanting him as badly as he'd once wanted her was very appealing.

Genie looked out the peephole. Alex Dalton. What was he doing here?

She turned on the porch light, unlocked the dead bolt and slowly opened the heavy wooden door. He was dressed in a ski sweater and twill pants, but looked just as striking as he had in denim and leather.

Genie felt dowdy in the outfit she'd worn to work and wished she'd changed. How could she have known that after so many lonely evenings, an attractive male would show up on her doorstep tonight? Of course anything else available for her to change into would have been as plain. All her clothes were chosen for their comfort at work.

Her occupation was only part of the reason for her changed appearance. Much was Will's doing. His admonitions that attractive clothes on her were false advertising had both consciously and unconsciously shaped her current wardrobe.

"Hello, Mr. Dalton. Wh—" She stopped abruptly. Remembering his comments from this afternoon, she decided it was best not to ask what she could do for him.

Alex smiled and flashed her a look of boyish innocence. "Hi. You look surprised to see me."

"Yes, I am."

"I came by to apologize for upsetting your student this afternoon."

It was a thoughtful gesture. "I, um, I should also apologize for being rude."

"It was a natural reaction. Just like a mama bear defending her cubs."

She tucked a stray wisp of hair behind her ear. "I'm not sure I like being compared to a bear."

"I could have said mother hen."

"That's even worse."

He sighed. The smile faded from his mouth but intensified in his eyes. "Then I guess I've blown my chances of being invited in."

Two

Even through the screen door Genie felt a jolt of awareness. The man was positively lethal! There was no way he could be the number-crunching math whiz who had gotten her through algebra.

"Mercy, where are my manners? Please come in." She deliberately exaggerated her drawl.

"Thank you."

Genie unlocked the screen door and pushed it open. Alex stepped past her into the living room.

"Would you like something to drink? Coffee? Ice tea? Lemonade?"

He turned and looked at her. "Do you make lemonade as good as your mother's?"

She sucked in her breath. "When have you had my mother's lemonade?"

He took a step forward, reached out one hand and tilted her chin up. "You don't remember me, do you, angel? I'm crushed." He released her and took a few steps back.

Looking at the handsome, ruggedly masculine features and well-built body, she once again failed to find any sign of the boy she'd known.

"I do remember an Alexander Dalton who used to visit Grandee during summer vacation, but..." How could she phrase this without insulting him? "He wasn't the blue jeans, leather jacket and motorcycle type."

"And you weren't the schoolmarm type, Genie."

It only hurt a little when her sister called her a schoolmarm, but hearing it from an attractive man was disheartening. "I always wanted to be a teacher. That's why it was so important for me to pass algebra so I could get into college."

"Ah, so you do remember."

"Then you are the same Alex?"

He raised his arms slightly, palms facing her. "Guilty as charged."

It was all she could do to keep her mouth from falling open. She'd heard the story of the ugly duckling many times, but considered it a wonderful piece of fiction. Things like that never happened in real life. Scruffy ducklings didn't grow up to be swans, and nerdy guys did not change into hunks. Metamorphosis was strictly for butterflies.

"Can I try the lemonade?"

"Yes, of course." Genie hurried into the kitchen. She fixed two glasses, picked them up and turned to head back to the living room.

Alex was leaning casually against the door frame, arms folded over his broad chest and one foot crossed over the other. Once again she was struck by how drop-dead gorgeous he was. She came close to dropping the lemonade, but Alex stepped forward and took the glasses from her shaky hands.

"I'll take those."

He stepped back, letting her slip past.

In the living room, she gathered up the homework papers she'd been grading and stacked them on the end table. Alex sat down on the floral print couch. Genie chose the matching love seat.

Sipping her drink, she looked cautiously at Alex, wondering if he'd only come by to apologize or if he had some other motive.

Sure, Genie, like this gorgeous hunk of male might want something else from you. In your dreams...

Alex tasted the lemonade. "Just as good as your mother made. How are your parents and your sister? Magnolia, wasn't it?"

"Yes. They're all fine." *Wait until Maggie got a look at Alex. She wouldn't believe her eyes, either.* She set her glass down on the end table and clasped her hands together, searching for something to say. "So, you live in New York?"

"Yes."

"Did you ride your motorcycle all that way?"

"I flew into Atlanta and picked up the bike there."

"Have you always lived in New York?"

It was the first time she'd wondered where he lived when he wasn't visiting Grandee. But when he'd been a regular summer visitor, she'd had a crush on Will Tucker and hadn't paid attention to any other males. In all honesty, though, even if she hadn't been with Will, she wouldn't have looked twice at Alex back then.

Alex took a long drink from his glass before answering. "No, I was born and raised in California."

"Was it your idea to come to Wiley every summer?" She couldn't imagine him wanting to come someplace where he was so unpopular, and so unhappy, if he'd had a choice.

"I loved to see Grandee, of course, but the trips were mostly for my parents' benefit. They're both professors at Cal Tech and between their research projects and their students they didn't have time to have me underfoot all summer."

"I would never have guessed California. But that does explain why you don't have a New York accent."

He laughed. "Grandee would probably refuse to speak to me if I did. She had a fit when I moved up there. Although she is getting used to the fact that I work for Yankee Motorworks. She's finally beginning to accept that the name helps identify the bike as an

American product on the international market and has nothing to do with the War Between the States."

"You work for Yankee Motorworks?" Genie didn't know much about motorcycles, but she'd heard of the company's phenomenal success and had seen the Yankee ad that was creating a stir around the country. The tabloids were having a field day trying to guess the identity of the three men, hidden behind full-face helmets, posing beside three motorcycles.

"Yes, the motorcycle company."

"You wouldn't work in the advertising department by any chance?"

He shook his head. "No, but I hired the firm that handles the advertising."

"Do you know who the models in the ad are?"

"I do."

"Who are they?"

The slow, sexy smile from this afternoon was back. He set his lemonade down and leaned farther into the cushions. "You could come here and try to bribe it out of me."

Genie hopped off the love seat. Hands on hips, she stood in front of him. "Does that line work with Yankee women?"

His smile tilted to one side, emphasizing his dimple and giving him a boyish look. "I haven't tried it, but I don't think they'd fall for it."

"That's a relief. Any woman with half the sense God gave a mule would throw you out on your cute little rump for that one."

She turned and headed for the door. She had expected him to follow, but once the door was open, she looked back and found him still sitting on the couch.

"Do you really mean it?"

"Yes, I do. I want you to leave."

He got up and walked over to stand in front of her. "I was sure you meant that, angel. But what I'd like to know is whether you really think I have a cute rump?"

He was just as precocious as her students, and she had to fight back a smile.

But then he took a step closer and the breath caught in her throat. Her gaze dropped to his mouth. He wasn't smiling anymore.

One more step and the distance between them shrank until they were just short of touching. He was going to kiss her. Instinctively she moved her hands up and set them on the hard wall of his chest, planning to push away. Instead she stayed where she was, tilting her head to look into his eyes.

Yes, he was going to kiss her... and she was not going to push him away. Lord help her, she was going to kiss him back.

One strong hand came up and curled around her neck, his fingers warm against her skin. She went up on tiptoe. Her eyes started to close.

Then Alex moved away, taking his warmth with him. Cool evening air swept over Genie.

"Night, angel," Alex said as he let himself out the screen door.

* * *

Alex shoved his hands into his pockets, walked down the front walk and out the gate in the white picket fence.

Genie had wanted him to kiss her. And for a moment there, he'd wanted to kiss her.

Kiss her and then some.

Standing close to her, his vision had blurred. For an instant it seemed he saw her the way he'd imagined she would look grown up. Strong desire had kicked through him. He'd wanted that image.

Dried leaves crunched beneath his feet as he continued down the sidewalk. There were a few new houses in what had been empty lots, and some of the old houses looked like they'd been refurbished. But essentially the streets of Wiley looked much the way they had when he'd been young.

Lights shone out the windows, and the scent of burning logs hung in the early autumn air.

A vision of himself and Genie, lying entwined in front of a crackling fire, flashed into his mind. Genie with her hair falling in soft waves over her bare shoulders, with a smile on her lips and a sparkle in her eye.

He was going to have her. But he was going to have to wait. Because he was going to make her wait.

Genie was going to wait. The payback would be much sweeter if he enticed her slowly, won over her emotions before taking her to bed.

The summer he'd tutored her, he would have sold his soul for one kiss from her. He'd wanted so much to ask her out. He'd even practiced asking. Back in the woods behind Grandee's house, palms sweating profusely, he'd sat on top of a flat rock and gone over it and over it.

"Eugenia, would you like to catch a movie with me?"

He'd almost had it down to where his voice didn't crack, when Will Tucker had come sneaking up behind him from deeper within the woods.

By the time Will had finished mocking and lambasting him, Alex had lost the courage to ask Genie out.

She probably would have given him the same you-must-be-kidding look he'd gotten the only other time he'd asked a girl out that year.

Or Genie might have laughed.

Or worse, she might have looked at him with pity. That would have hurt more than the other kids' deliberate cruelty.

Let the memories rest, Alex. It's all over, all in the past. And the past belonged behind him.

What would Genie have said if he'd told her that he was one of the mystery men in the Yankee ads? That he, Jesse and Rorke had posed for the photos.

Did it matter that she would have turned him down when they'd been in high school? Tonight she'd wanted him to kiss her. He imagined her curled up on her flowery feminine couch, her mouth aching for the touch of his.

When he headed back to New York, he would leave her aching for a whole lot more.

* * *

Genie leaned against the closed front door. Slowly her heartbeat and breathing returned to normal. Her mind tumbled through the last few minutes, reliving what had happened.

What had *almost* happened . . .

She'd been sure he was going to kiss her. And she'd wanted to be kissed. She hadn't kissed anyone since Will. Hadn't wanted to kiss anyone since Will.

But tonight she'd wanted Alex's kiss. She'd wanted to press close to his hard warmth and feel his mouth coming down over hers.

He'd outraged her with his suggestion that she try to bribe him. But since he hadn't kissed her when he'd had the chance, he must have been teasing. Like a love-starved schoolmarm, she'd overreacted.

Overreacted because the thought of joining him on the couch had appealed to her more than she'd been willing to admit. She admitted it now, but felt uneasy.

She pushed away from the door, walked into the kitchen and picked up the phone. Her older sister answered on the third ring.

They talked about Maggie's two children and Genie's students until Maggie said, "What's bugging you, Genie? Get it off your chest."

"I'm not sure I want to talk about it."

"Did you see Will on TV again? When are you going to get over him?"

Genie never deliberately turned on a football game, but occasionally she would accidently catch Will on a sports report or a commercial. She usually called her sister afterward.

"Maggie, I was in love with him forever and engaged to him for four years. My feelings aren't going to just disappear." Except maybe they were starting to. Maybe that was why she'd felt attracted to Alex. Maybe that was why she was feeling out of sync. "But that's not why I called. Do you remember Alex Dalton?"

"Did he go to school with us?"

"No, he stayed with Grandee in the summer."

"That tall, skinny kid nobody would play with?"

"That's the one. He's here for her birthday."

Genie told her the story about Joey and Paul. Then how Alex had come over to her house, how she'd wanted to kiss him...

"I can't believe he didn't follow through. I mean how many offers can the poor guy get?"

"I'd say he probably has more than he can handle."

Maggie laughed. "He must look different than he did."

Genie described him as she'd seen him this afternoon.

"Big, black motorcycle? Was it a Yankee?"

"Probably. He works for the company."

"That was Alex Dalton?"

"You saw him?"

"I think so. I saw a to-die-for blond biker at the gas station this afternoon. Sky blue eyes... a smile that wouldn't quit..."

"This from a happily married woman?"

"I can't believe you had him in your house and let him get away before morning."

Genie knew her sister was teasing, but the joke hit too close to home. "That's part of the problem, the idea is appealing. And this is the first time I've felt like this about any man other than Will."

"And it's about time. Go for it. Just be sure to use safe sex."

Genie laughed. "He flirted, but when the moment came, he didn't even kiss me."

"You probably put up your schoolmarm facade and scared him away."

She looked at her skirt and reached up with her free hand and tugged at her bun. She hadn't put on her schoolmarm facade and scared Alex.

She'd become the schoolmarm facade.

No wonder he hadn't kissed her. "I wanted him to kiss me. It was a strange feeling."

"A normal, healthy feeling. Welcome back to life, Genie."

"Nobody staying after school today, Miss Hill?"

Genie spun around to find Alex standing in the open doorway. Maggie's description of him last night immediately came to mind—a to-die-for blond biker. "No, nobody after school."

"No spiders in lunch boxes?"

She set down the eraser she was holding and walked to her desk, standing behind it. Hiding as much of today's conservative outfit as possible. "None that the lunchroom monitor told me about."

Alex came farther into the room. A hot heaviness swept through Genie's lower body as she watched him walk toward her. He looked like a predator stalking his prey. But if that was true, then he wouldn't have left last night with just a verbal good-night.

"My grandmother tells me you're in charge of the decorations for Grandee's birthday party."

"Yes, I've ordered balloons, fresh floral arrangements, and the Wiley Women's Club is making some silk flower centerpieces and—"

"You might want to make a few changes. We're switching the location."

"It's not going to be at the Women's Club?"

"There's not room for all the guests and the media inside the Women's Club."

She crossed her arms over her chest. "That's why we're setting up tables outside, too. And besides, we weren't planning on tables for the media."

"You get better press if you roll out the red carpet for the media. As for the tables outside, as the evening wears on, it's going to get cold. And what if it should rain?"

"What do you suggest we do then?" She wanted to tell him that a lot of people had put in a lot of time planning this party. Who was he to just ride in one day and start undoing all their hard work?

"I've rented Roseleigh."

"Roseleigh?"

Roseleigh Plantation was five miles outside Wiley town limits. It was a private residence, and the ballroom was occasionally rented by movie makers for use in films. More often, though, it was rented for weddings.

From the day she'd visited Roseleigh on a school field trip, she'd dreamed of having her wedding there. A candlelight ceremony in the grand ballroom, followed by dinner and dancing.

"You only turn a hundred once," Alex said, breaking into her thoughts.

"But I'm sure there isn't enough in the party budget..."

"It's not coming out of the budget. It's part of my gift. In addition, I'll cover the cost of any extra decorations you want to order or hire someone to come in and take care of them, if you'd like."

The decorations would have a more polished look if she let him hire someone. She wasn't a professional, although she did have flair. And was often called upon to head the decorating committee for a variety of functions.

"The decorations have been a group effort. Besides the Women's Club, the students and the VFW have all been making things."

A professional probably wouldn't want to use the handmade place cards, name tags, napkin rings and banners—but would these things look out of place in the elegance of Roseleigh?

"Well, then, why don't we ride out there and you can take a look around?"

"I, um…" Did she want to spend the afternoon with Alex, considering the attraction she'd felt for him last night? Especially since Roseleigh was an emotionally charged place for her? Besides, she had papers to grade. But the party was on Sunday, and if she needed to change the flowers… "All right."

"Then get home and into your blue jeans."

The notion that she'd rather get into *his* stunned her, and all she managed to do was echo his words, "Blue jeans?"

"You can't wear a dress on a motorcycle."

"Motorcycle?"

Three

————

Genie had never ridden on the back of a motorcycle. The experience wasn't what she had imagined it would be. She was afraid to think of the open air around her. But that was nothing compared to the distraction of being pressed against Alex's back.

At first it was comforting to lean into his warm strength and wrap her arms around him. She felt protected and sheltered. Then the feelings changed, and there was nothing safe or secure about them.

The vibrations of the powerful engine hummed through her. And every move Alex made echoed along her nerve endings.

Movements of his left leg when he shifted, or his right leg when he applied the rear brake, sent sensations racing along the inside of her thighs. She felt the movements of his arms in the expanding and contracting of the muscles in his back.

By the time they reached the long, oak-flanked driveway leading to Roseleigh, Genie was a mass of awakened desire.

From the sly smile on Alex's face when he helped her take off the helmet, she knew her feelings must be written all over her face.

"How did you like it?"

She'd liked it too much, but wasn't about to tell him so. "It was fine."

"Just fine?" His smile became a grin.

"Well, it was pleasant with the Indian summer temperatures, but I'm not sure I'd like it in colder weather."

"I'm strictly a fair-weather rider. But there are some die-hards who bundle up and stay on two wheels until the first freeze." He set the helmet she'd been wearing next to his. "Are you sure this was your first time riding?"

"Yes."

"Then you're a natural. You were right with me the whole time."

"Of course I was with you. Did you think I'd gotten off at the first stop sign?"

He quirked one brow. "Why, Genie, I believe you do still have a sense of humor. I'd begun to wonder. What I meant was that you didn't fight me or the bike on turns and curves like most first timers do."

Genie wondered how many first-time riders Alex had initiated. How many other women had sat behind him and been aroused by his every movement? And how often had he followed through and satisfied the needs he'd triggered?

"Shall we go in?" Alex led her up the steps and onto the wide veranda of the white-columned Greek Revival mansion.

White wicker furniture with floral print cushions invited visitors to sit and look out over the spacious manicured front lawn and watch the breeze-tossed Spanish moss swing from the branches of the stately oaks, or look beyond the road and watch the sun set behind the Appalachian Mountains against the far horizon.

One of the oversize front doors opened, and a woman peered out, upsetting the mood.

Alex had apparently been to the house before because the housekeeper knew him by name. After he introduced Genie, they were shown to the ballroom and left alone.

"Well, what do you think?"

Ornate plasterwork, gilt-framed mirrors, elaborate sconces, crystal chandeliers, polished wood floors, French doors... "It's beautiful." But once again she worried about whether their simple handmade decorations would fit in. They would probably look as out of place as a small-town Georgia girl on the arm of an NFL quarterback.

"You don't seem pleased."

"It's just that the Women's Center has a warmer, quainter atmosphere." And no ghostly memories from her young dreams of herself in white, dancing with Will on their wedding day.

"The room's empty now. It will look different with the tables set up."

Tables with cloth covers, china, crystal and matching silver, no doubt. "Even with tables it's just so…so formal. The town's functions are always held in the Women's Center, and it serves us just fine."

"From what I hear, Roseleigh has been used quite often by people from Wiley for weddings."

She shrugged. "This isn't a wedding. It's a birthday party. This is too glitzy for a birthday party."

He planted his fists on his hips. "Thank you for your opinion, Miss Hill."

"And what about the distance from town? Many people were probably planning on walking to the party. Especially the older folks who don't like to drive after dark."

"I've chartered buses to shuttle guests back and forth from the town square."

He had an answer for everything. She would have been impressed if she wasn't so upset about him switching the location. In her experience, last-minute changes usually caused more problems than they were worth—except for the person making them.

Her father had run roughshod over her young years—always overturning any plans she, Maggie or their mother had made to suit his needs. Every aspect of their life revolved around his hardware store.

She'd hated it, yet turned around and let Will and his goal to play professional ball move in and control her. While they'd been together, she'd only been able to work as a substitute teacher, and then only when the team was scheduled for home play. He wanted her with him on the road, even though he left her to occupy herself for long periods of time. But she was expected to be at his beck and call.

Genie realized suddenly how much she'd enjoyed the independence and freedom of the last few years.

Alex broke into her thoughts. "Can you handle the decorating or would you like me to hire someone?"

"What about Grandee's feelings? How do you know she wouldn't rather have her party in Wiley?"

"I ran the idea by my grandmother, and she thought it was fine. Besides, I lived with my great-grandmother three months of every year for a large part of my life. I think that should give me a pretty good idea of what would please her."

"And you think having her birthday party here would please her?"

"Yes, I do." He crossed his arms over his chest. "She met my great-grandfather here at Roseleigh."

"Oh. I didn't know." If Roseleigh had sentimental meaning for Grandee, maybe she would rather have her party here.

But there was no way Genie was going to let everyone's hard work be for nothing. Amateurish or not, the artistic offerings of the people of Wiley were going to grace the ballroom at Roseleigh.

She looked around again, trying to erase the vision of the room set up for her wedding by picturing it ready for the birthday party. Bright, vibrant colors. Not a pastel hue in sight—balloons, brightly wrapped gifts.

Would it be enough to erase the unfulfilled visions from her memory?

"It might work," she muttered, talking more to herself than Alex.

Alex congratulated himself on being right. Genie looked much better in blue jeans than her schoolteacher clothes. And from the feel of her behind him on the bike, he could tell she would look damned good without them, too.

Now if she would just let her hair down, both literally and figuratively.

She'd agreed to handle the changes in the decorations. But she still seemed opposed to Grandee's party being at Roseleigh. He couldn't understand why. But whatever her reasons, he seemed to be the villain in her mind.

When she climbed onto the motorcycle for the trip to Wiley, she was stiff and tight, holding herself away from him. He considered pulling over and forcing the issue, but once they were off the straight driveway and on the curving road, the tilt of the bike rocked her forward. He felt the tension drain from her muscles and her body relax against him.

The thought of holding her face-to-face and feeling the same reaction created an unwanted tension in part of his body. A part in easy reach of the small feminine hands clasped around his middle.

If only she would slide her hands down and . . .

Whoa, pal!

He couldn't get them home safely if he let his mind wander any farther in that direction.

Instead, he pushed his thoughts to his last summer in Wiley, the summer he'd tutored Genie. He'd already mentally relived the humiliation of his encounter with Will in the woods, but now he let himself remember an incident that had occurred a week later.

After he and Genie had finished with the day's lesson—factoring polynomials—Mrs. Hill came into the room and invited him to Genie's birthday party the following Friday evening.

He was excited by the invitation and had every intention of going.

After leaving for the day, he got half a block away before deciding to go back and ask Mrs. Hill for gift ideas. If he could find out what Genie wanted most, maybe he could outdo Will. . . .

The raised voices were audible the moment he reached the porch. They were coming from an open window upstairs. He raised his arm to knock on the screen door, but then he heard what Mrs. Hill said.

"I thought he might enjoy socializing with people his own age for a change."

"I can't believe you're doing this to me! I'll be a laughingstock."

Mrs. Hill's voice lowered in volume, but he could still hear her words. "The other kids may like him once they get to know him."

"Sure, Mom, when pigs fly." Genie had also stopped yelling.

"You two seem to get along during your tutoring sessions."

"Oh, he's a great tutor. He's smart and really knows his stuff. But he not only knows the stuff, he likes it. Can you believe it?" She laughed. "What a nerd."

"Eugenia Grace Hill," her mother started, but Alex didn't stay to hear the rest of the conversation. He'd heard enough. More than enough.

And here they were, years later, ro—ng down the road, pressed together from shoulders to knees.

He wished he could go back to the teenager he'd been, shuffling home with Genie's voice repeating, "What a nerd." Over and over again in his mind.

If he could go back, he would pat himself on the shoulder and tell himself not to worry or agonize over Genie's rejection.

He would tell the young Alex that Genie would take back her words. That she would let him—no, make that *beg* him—to do all the things he'd fantasized about doing to her in his youthful dreams.

As well as a few things he'd learned later.

For Genie, the ride to town was even more disturbing than the ride out had been. They wound their way into the foothills as the late afternoon shadows lengthened. She started out appreciating the scenery, but then her mind and body focused only on the man in front of her.

The engine downshifted to a steady idle as they came to a stop. When she got off the bike, she was grateful to be putting some space between them. She started to thank Alex for the ride, then realized they weren't parked at her house as she'd expected them to be, but were in front of the Wiley Café.

Genie looked at Alex, one brow raised in question.

"I thought we could have dinner before I took you home."

"That's not necessary. I have papers to grade, and I'm sure you'd rather visit with your family."

"I'll get you home right after dinner. Just think of the time you'll save not having to cook."

He had a point. But sharing a table with a man she was so physically attracted to might prove too big a challenge.

It turned out to be even more challenging to ignore the covert glances and blatant stares from the staff and other customers. A number of people stopped by the booth where she and Alex were sitting. Since most of their peers greeted him by name, Genie surmised that word had already spread about his being in town and how his appearance had changed.

Over dinner, she and Alex talked about her students, including the rambunctious Joey and Paul.

"You seem to enjoy your job," he said.

"I do. How about you? Do you like your job?"

"I love it, but it keeps me exceptionally busy."

"What do you do at Yankee besides hire advertising firms?"

"Make decisions and delegate."

"So, you're in management?"

"I'm the CEO and one of the founders."

Genie was glad she'd already swallowed her sip of ice tea before Alex had spoken. "CEO? As in chief executive officer?"

"Yes."

"I've never had dinner with a CEO before."

"Then we're even. I've never had dinner with an elementary schoolteacher."

He probably had dinner with exciting New York women, women on the corporate fast track, actresses, models. More than likely she'd been boring him silly with talk of her students.

She had no idea what to say next, but was saved when Skip Evans, one of Will's old friends, walked up to their table.

"Evenin', Genie."

"Skip." Genie acknowledged his greeting while watching Skip stare at Alex. "I believe you know Alex Dalton. He used to visit during the summer."

Skip's eyes opened wider. "Well, I'll be. I thought Casey was pulling my leg."

Genie supposed Skip had asked the waitress, Casey, about Alex.

"Nice to see you again, Skip," Alex said. His voice sounded polite, but Genie noticed the usual warm undertones were missing.

"I guess you're here for the big to-do for Grandee."

"Yes."

"Skip, your order's up," Casey hollered across the room.

Skip shrugged. "Chow time. I'll see y'all around." He turned and walked away.

"It seems like most of the people I remember from my visits still live in Wiley," Alex said.

Genie noticed he'd used the word *people*. The *people* he remembered, rather than friends. She looked back on how the summers must have been for Alex.

She felt a twinge of guilt that she hadn't been more friendly to him then. "Most of them do. A few of the girls moved away when they got married, but most of the guys have settled down here in town, either in their family's businesses or opened a business of their own."

"Except Will."

Genie froze at her ex-fiancé's name. "His father still expects to have him at the gas station someday."

"Do you think it'll happen?"

Normally she would try to change the subject when anyone asked about Will, but this evening she found herself answering. "I don't think so. Will talked about becoming an announcer or a coach when his days on the field are over."

"That will be a while. I'm sure he has a long successful career ahead of him."

"Are you a football fan?"

"No, I rarely watch it. But I could tell that Will would make a great quarterback by the way he threw water balloons. Long, arched and right on target."

She hadn't realized Alex and Will had ever been friends. "When did you and Will throw water balloons together?"

"We never threw them together. I was one of his favorite targets."

Genie wondered if that had anything to do with the way he'd reacted when Joey had hit him with a water balloon.

"Do you see him at all?" Alex asked.

Was the trip to Roseleigh and dinner just a ploy to get to Will? "Why? Do you want me to get you game tickets?" It was a common request. People seemed to think that because they'd been engaged, she could call Will anytime and ask for favors.

"Seems I've hit a raw nerve." He pushed his coffee cup to the side of the table, then scooted hers over and took her hand in his, twining their fingers together. "What I want is to know why the two of you broke up and what kind of relationship you currently have. And not because I'm interested in Will. But because I'm interested in you."

He was interested in her? In what way? As an old friend? But they'd never been friends...only acquaintances. She was only one of the people he remembered.

With her free hand she took her napkin out of her lap, folded it and set it on the table. "I don't see why you'd be interested."

Alex moved his hand slightly, sending tingling sparks up her arm. "You're an attractive, single woman, and I'm a healthy single male."

Attractive? Did he really think she was attractive, or was that his standard line? If he was attracted to her, wouldn't he have followed through with the kiss last night? Besides, ultimately what did it matter? He was only going to be here a short time. "A healthy, single male on vacation."

He shrugged. "Is there a problem with that?"

Genie was intensely aware of the warmth of his hand against hers, its strength and size. She envisioned what it would feel like to have his hands touching more sensitive parts of her body. "I'm not looking for a fast fling."

"What are you looking for?"

The question stunned her. She'd always pictured herself living in Wiley with a husband and children in a house very similar to the one she now lived in alone. But since she'd moved back, she'd concentrated on living each day, not thinking more than a few weeks ahead. She looked at her empty coffee cup. "I don't know what I'm looking for."

Her gaze moved to Alex.

He was looking at her intently, somewhere short of a frown, but he quickly flashed her one of his heart-stopping smiles. "Then how do you know you're not looking for a fast fling?"

Genie was speechless.

"And if you're going to do it," Alex continued, "you'd be better off with someone you don't have to worry about running into around town."

He made it sound like a cool, logical decision. But there was nothing cool going on throughout her body, starting with where her hand rested in Alex's.

The unsettling thoughts of an unfulfilling future narrowed as her attention turned to visions of what he was offering her for the next few hours. "I, um . . ."

"Say yes, angel. You know you want to."

The specter of not knowing what she wanted from the future fled completely in response to Alex's lethal charm. She smiled. "I'll bet you could sweet-talk the birds from the trees."

"I'd rather sweet-talk you into my arms."

If he knew how close he was to succeeding, she'd be in big trouble.

"Y'all want a refill on coffee?" Casey asked.

"Genie?" Alex gave her hand a brief squeeze before letting it go.

She shook her head.

"We'll have the check," Alex said to Casey.

After settling the bill, Alex led Genie out front to where they'd left the bike. Just looking at it made the soft, sensitive skin of her inner thighs tingle with the memory of resting alongside Alex.

She looked at him. The flare of desire in his eyes burned right through her. If they were in a private secluded place, she knew she wouldn't be able to resist the invitation he offered. She knew she'd be safer walking home.

But once Alex was on the bike, holding his hand out to her, she got on behind him and settled herself against his back.

It was only a mile.

Half a block down the road, her breasts felt tight and achy. Pressing more securely against Alex relieved some of the discomfort, but the benefit was lost when he adjusted his position.

It seemed like no time at all before Alex turned smoothly into her driveway. What would the neighbors think if the bike was still parked there in the morning? she wondered. What would Alex think if she asked him to put it in the garage?

Hold the phone, Genie. The man is not staying. Thank him for dinner and send him on his way...

She hopped off the bike and headed up the drive. "Thank you for dinner. I had a lovely time."

She heard the click of his kickstand, then the tread of his boots following her. After opening the side gate in her fence, she continued up the walkway to her front porch. By the time she reached the door, Alex was right behind her.

"In a hurry, Genie?"

Four

"**I** told you earlier that I have papers to correct."

Alex's hands came down and rested on her shoulders. "They can't wait a few more minutes?"

"Well..."

Slowly, he turned her around. With only the glow from the streetlight out front, she couldn't read his expression entirely, but she saw well enough to know he wanted to kiss her.

Maybe he'll stop at the last moment again.

Would she be able to survive if he did? She'd probably chase after him and take him down into the geraniums. After the sensation of riding behind him, she had to know what it felt like to be in his arms with his mouth on hers.

He reached out and gathered her to him. Leaning forward, she realized his chest was as warm and hard as his back, but even more inviting. She snuggled close, then tilted her head to look at him.

It was all the prompting he seemed to need.

He brought his mouth down over hers. The movement was tentative at first. Tentative but skillful. A soft sigh escaped her lips, and Alex started to pull back. Genie opened her mouth to protest and he was there again, deepening the kiss, exploring the warm sensitive recesses of her mouth with his tongue.

She followed his lead, returning the kiss with all the yearning that had been building throughout the afternoon and evening.

It was sweet relief. It was magic. Total magic, rocking her all the way to her toes.

Alex stopped the kiss, but he didn't let her go. He pulled her closer, his breath warm against her neck as he held her for long, quiet moments.

The leather of his jacket creaked as he loosened his hold and straightened to his full height. "Night, angel." He turned and started to walk away.

No kiss had ever affected her like that. Shouldn't she tell him . . . or ask if he'd felt the same? "Alex?"

He stopped, but didn't turn around. "Don't suggest coffee unless you intend it to be with breakfast."

"I just wanted to say good-night."

"Good night." He continued on his way.

Genie let herself in. She leaned against the closed door until she heard the motorcycle engine roar to life.

Her steps were wobbly as she headed up the stairs. Once she reached her bedroom, she flipped on the light.

She looked around the room, seeing it as she imagined Alex would. It was obviously a woman's room, full of frills. Her gaze moved across the polished hardwood floors to the quilt-draped brass bed. Even with the collection of ruffle-and-lace throw pillows inviting her in, the bed seemed strangely empty tonight.

Alex hung up the phone more forcefully than necessary. Jesse wasn't home. Or maybe he just wasn't answering the phone.

His other partner, Rorke O'Neil, had recently gotten married so the chances of reaching him were better. And he needed to talk to one of them.

Alex dialed. The phone rang twice before it was answered by a feminine voice, warm with sleep.

"Hi, beautiful. How's the weather?"

"Alex?" Callie asked. "Do you know what time it is?"

"About eleven. Is Rorke around?"

"He's right here."

There was a short pause, then, "This had better be important, Dalton," Rorke said.

Yes, it was important, his peace of mind had been rattled by Genie's kiss. "Have you ever kissed a woman...just kissed her...a fully clothed and vertical kiss...but walked away feeling like you'd made love to her for hours?"

Rorke laughed. "I know just what you mean."

"Great, I thought I was losing my mind."

"You're not losing your mind, pal, but you can kiss your freedom goodbye."

"My freedom?"

"I've only had that kind of experience with one woman, Alex."

Oh, no. A tight knot formed in Alex's stomach. "Callie?" The word was a harsh whisper.

"None other."

Alex collected his composure. Lose his freedom? No way. He had too many lost years to make up for. "Don't worry. I'm not about to give up my freedom."

"Then I suggest you stay away from this woman."

It would be difficult to seduce Genie and stay away from her at the same time. His plan for revenge was going well, he knew he would win, and he wasn't about to walk away because her kisses hadn't been what he'd expected.

He hoped forewarned really was forearmed. "Thanks for the warning."

Rorke laughed. "Hey, marriage isn't that bad. In fact there's a lot to be said for it."

Alex heard Callie chuckle in the background. "Say good night to Callie for me and tell her I'm sorry I woke her."

"I'll make it up to her."

"You do that."

"Don't be surprised if she calls and thanks you in the morning."

Alex chuckled as he hung up the phone. At least someone would have a deep, restful sleep tonight.

Rorke seemed happier since his marriage. But he had probably been ready to settle down when he'd caved in to the big commitment.

Besides, Rorke and Callie had only recently married, but they'd first fallen in love ten years ago.

Alex could see himself ready to be married in ten years or so.

Tonight, Genie's hot kisses might have taken him by surprise, but he wasn't about to let them threaten his freedom.

Genie checked her messages at the beginning of her lunch period—faculty meeting after school, PTA drive results and a note for her to call her sister.

"Maggie, what's up?"

"That's what I called to find out. I hear you were out with Alex Dalton last night."

"Not exactly."

"Casey said you two had dinner together at the café."

"We did, but it wasn't exactly a date." She explained about the trip to Roseleigh and stopping for dinner afterward.

"Casey said it looked pretty cozy. She said you two were holding hands and gazing into each other's eyes."

Was that how it had looked? What must people have been thinking? Were they thinking that a good-looking man like Alex must have a screw loose to be out with her?

"Did he spend the night?"

"Maggie!"

"Did he at least kiss you this time?"

Genie sighed. It was useless to lie. One of the neighbors had probably seen them and would be spreading the word anyway.

"Yes, he kissed me good night."

"Yowza."

"Was that all you wanted? If so I'd like to grab something to eat before my lunch break is over."

"That's all for now, but I'll want a full report later."

Genie groaned as she hung up the phone. A full report...there were dozens of things she'd rather do than tell Maggie about the kiss she'd shared with Alex.

First and foremost, she'd like a second round of kisses.

Alex did everything he could to keep busy—so busy he wouldn't have time to think about Genie. He had his notebook computer, cellular phone and fax machine with him so he spent most of the day working.

After dinner, Grandee was heading out to play bridge and he was left wondering what he would do that evening when his cousin Donny called and invited him to play pool at the Dixie Lounge.

Donny hadn't wanted anything to do with him when they'd been younger—in fact, if he remembered correctly, Donny was the one who had called him "Specs" the first time.

But if he didn't find something to keep himself busy, he would be tempted to call Genie and ask to see her this evening. If she agreed, he knew he would be tempted to kiss her again. And if it was anything like the first time, he would be tempted to keep right on going until he had her naked beneath him.

It was too soon . . , she hadn't waited long enough.

There was a familiar heat and tightening going on, but he ignored it. Alex could handle a little discomfort if it meant Genie would feel a small taste of the frustration he'd gone through night after night that long-ago summer.

Tossing, turning and thinking about the way her tongue would slip out to wet her lips when she was considering an algebra problem or the way she would shift in her chair, stretching the muscles of her back, making him even more aware of her developing female curves. . . . He remembered every torturous detail of those hours he'd spent with her, but dwelling on them now would only worsen his current physical condition.

He rode the Yankee slowly through town and then beyond until he reached the Dixie. He'd passed by it many times, but never stopped.

It was a typical small-town establishment, a bar that served beer or soda, three well-used pool tables, an assortment of small round tables, a jukebox with a wide selection of music as long as you liked country and western and a small sawdust-covered dance floor at the far end of the long room.

"Alex!"

He turned to see Donny waving to him from the center pool table. Everyone seemed glad to see him and asked questions about Yankee Motorworks and the bike he'd brought to town.

He managed to banish Genie from his thoughts and was having a good time after winning a few games. Then Alex noticed a man leaning against the bar watching him with narrowed eyes as he sipped on a long-neck beer. It only took him a few moments to come up with a name for the sullen face...Kenny Tucker, Will's younger brother.

After finishing his beer and leaving the bottle on the bar, Kenny ambled over to stand next to Alex. Once they were side by side, Alex realized how short the other man was. He'd dated women taller. Kenny barely reached his shoulder.

"I hear you took Genie Hill out last night."

"That's right."

"Not a wise move. She's Will's woman."

"I heard they broke up."

"Yeah, they did temporarily. But he'll be settling down here someday, and they'll get back together."

"Just where did you hear this?"

"Will told me himself last time he was here."

Alex wondered if someone had called Will about last night. "And when was that?"

"Hell, about a month or so ago, I think."

"Apparently he never bothered to tell Genie. She's under the impression their relationship is over."

"It doesn't matter what she thinks. We all know she's off limits. And if you know what's good for you, city boy, you'll stay away from her, too."

Alex wasn't sure if he wanted to laugh or pick Kenny up by the scruff of his neck and tell him exactly what he thought of him and his warning. "Is that a threat?"

"No, that's a promise."

"Just what are you going to do if I take her out? Gather up your buddies, hide behind a tree and throw water balloons at me?"

"Let's just say we might have to arrange a makeshift nose job."

The sound of Donny's laughter caught Alex's attention, and he turned to look at his cousin.

"You'd need a stepladder to get anywhere near his nose, Kenny," Donny said.

Alex looked at the man in front of him. Had he grown so much more than Kenny after high school, or had he always been taller?

Had the boys who'd made his summers hell seemed larger than they'd actually been? Well, the pint-size bully might have made him jump through hoops as a kid, but no more.

"As long as there's no ring on her finger, I'd say Genie Hill is available to go out with any man she chooses. At the moment that's me."

Who did Will Tucker think he was? Sticking Genie in exile that way, an exile enforced by his brother and who else?

No matter, Alex would spend his free time in Wiley with Genie. Maybe by the time he left, with his nose intact, the other men in town would get up the courage to go against Will.

He liked the idea that he could kill two birds with one stone—following through on his plans with Genie and at the same time thumbing his nose at Will.

"Is it your birthday, Miss Hill?" several students asked.

"No." She was about to ask why, but catching sight of the delivery man with a large bouquet coming through the door, she understood.

"Who are they from? Who are they from?"

Genie suspected they might be from Alex. All day yesterday she'd expected to hear from him, but hadn't. She'd worried that she'd come on too strong when he'd kissed her, but she'd followed his lead and the yearning within her.

Then she'd worried that the kiss must not have been as wonderful for him as it had for her. Maybe she didn't live up to his standards . . . she hadn't been able to live up to Will's.

She'd given herself to Will with all the love in her heart. Apparently that hadn't been enough. His words about how disappointing he found her in bed still caused her pain. Especially since he'd waited four years to tell her. Waited until after she'd sacrificed her time and energy to their relationship—after she'd planned every detail of their wedding.

But maybe Will had kissed someone and felt the way she had with Alex...

Maybe the comfortable warmth and security she'd felt in the beginning with Will wasn't what making love was all about.

Maybe that's why Will had looked elsewhere.

Maybe she needed to look elsewhere...

She reached down and pulled out the small card buried among the blossoms. She smiled. Alex had sent the flowers.

"They're from a friend, children." It took a few minutes to get them settled down and focused on fractions.

Throughout the rest of the day, every time she caught a whiff of the flowers, or spotted them from the corner of her eye, her thoughts turned to Alex.

She wasn't surprised to see him standing in her door after school. But she was caught off guard by the shiny red apple he was tossing up and catching.

He smiled and her heart turned a somersault.

"Hi, Miss Hill. Can I come in?"

She smiled back. "Thank you for the flowers, Alex. They're beautiful."

He walked over to her desk and set the apple down in front of her. "This is for you, too. I thought you might need some sustenance after putting up with a room full of nine-year-olds."

Actually she felt more at ease with a room full of nine-year-olds than she did with this one full-grown male. "Flowers and an apple all in one day."

"While you're on a roll, how does taking in a movie sound?"

"I..." She hadn't frightened him off or failed to pass muster, after all. She fought back the urge to laugh, or hug him.

"I know it's short notice, and if you've already made other plans I'll understand. Although I'd rather you canceled them."

"I don't have any other plans."

"Great, I'll pick you up at seven then."

Last night hadn't been a date. Tonight would be. Butterflies quivered in Genie's stomach as she got ready for the evening ahead.

After her shower, she left her hair down for the first time in months. She put on a touch of makeup and sprayed on some of the perfume that had been sitting unused on her dresser.

The choice of slacks was easy, but she went around and around on the sweater. She usually wore a blouse under it or tucked a scarf into the open V of the neckline.

Tonight she tried it on with nothing more than a gold chain. There was more bare skin than she was used to seeing these days. She reached for her blouse, then stopped.

Alex had told her he was borrowing his grandparents' car so they didn't have to worry about facing the cold night air on the back of his motorcycle. She would be warm enough.

Sure, Genie. As if cold air is what you're really worrying about here.

Worrying about the cold, even worrying about wearing something he might find attractive was less bothersome than her most pressing question. Could she sit next to him in the close confines of a car and pretend the kiss hadn't happened? Pretend her lips weren't aching for him to do it again?

The doorbell rang at precisely seven o'clock. Once they were seated side by side in the car, Genie said, "I'll bet it seems strange driving a car after riding a motorcycle."

"It always does at first, but you adjust the same way you do going from a shift to an automatic car."

"Have you been riding long?"

"I started in graduate school. When Rorke and Jesse approached me about joining them in Yankee, I decided I should have firsthand experience with the product." He signaled for a right turn into the gas station.

Genie was surprised. The gas gauge was only down a quarter of a tank. The drive to and from the theater was only a mile, at most.

Unless he planned a long drive later? Like up to the lake?

No, that was ridiculous. Why would he take her to Lake Wiley? The place would be full of teenagers parking. It didn't seem like so long ago since one of the cars had held her and Will.

Put Will out of your mind. It's over. Concentrate on the man next to you.

Alex.

Alex who set her pulse racing and awoke a pounding desire in her.

Alex who would be leaving soon...

Besides, he wouldn't need to take her up to Lake Wiley to seduce her. She lived alone. He could seduce her right at her house.

So, why was it necessary to fill the gas tank?

Five

———

Alex pulled into the full-service lane and turned off the engine.

Kenny Tucker strolled up to the driver's window. He tilted his head and glanced at Genie before looking at Alex. "Fill 'er up?"

"Yes."

Kenny stepped to the pump. Alex slid his arm across the back of the seat so it rested behind her shoulders. "How are Joey and Paul doing?"

"Fine." She told him about Paul bursting into the office saying the Terminator had Joey and repeated the conversation that had followed Alex's leaving. He chuckled in all the right places, but she sensed Kenny had more of Alex's attention than she did. "Then they sprouted wings and flew home," she finished.

"Cute kids," Alex said, confirming her suspicion. His eyes turned to the back window again, then his gaze dropped to her mouth.

With no warning he closed the distance between them and kissed her. Genie forgot to worry about where they were and who might be watching, and kissed him back. Surrendering to the warmth and strength of his assault.

She wrapped her arms around his neck and leaned into him, sighing softly as his tongue slipped between her parted lips to tangle with hers.

This was what she had been craving from the moment their last kiss ended. Only now could she face how unhappy she'd been with the thought that their first kiss might also have been their last.

But it hadn't been. He was kissing her again.

She stored away every detail to think about later— the skilled pressure of his lips on hers, the seductive play of his tongue across the roof of her mouth, the warm taste of him, the erratic pounding of her heart, the tightness in her chest forcing her to take short shallow breaths, the tingling rhythmic throbbing deep within her.

At the intrusive sound of someone clearing his throat, Alex released her and turned.

Kenny was glaring in at them. "Hardly seems worth the stop for a few gallons."

Alex pulled out his wallet and paid Kenny. "When I borrow someone's car, I like to return it with a full tank."

"So y'all are on your way home."

"No, we're on the way out. But you'll be closed by the time I return the car. Unless—" Alex paused. "What time do you open in the morning?"

Genie could feel tension flowing back and forth between the two men. She wondered what was causing it. Something left over from when they were young? Or had something happened since Alex arrived in town?

Kenny's eyes narrowed and his face turned red. "We open at seven," he said through clenched teeth.

Alex nodded and smiled. "I'll keep that in mind for future reference."

The two men continued staring at each other. Genie suspected the trip to the station had more to do with Kenny than with Alex's wish to return the car with a full tank of gas.

With a sick, sinking feeling, she admitted the kiss that had meant so much to her had probably been for Kenny's benefit, too.

In the darkened movie theater, Alex's attention was more on the woman beside him than on the action taking place on the screen. Genie had been quiet since they'd left the gas station, and he was certain the kiss was to blame.

Way to go, Dalton.

He'd had more finesse the first time he'd kissed a woman than he'd shown in the car. It was as if all the savvy he'd developed over the last few years had completely disappeared.

He'd been so focused on Kenny, he couldn't have said what they'd been talking about just beforehand even if there was money riding on it.

What on earth was wrong with him?

Genie had responded to the kiss, but she'd looked puzzled when they'd left the station. And she hadn't said more than a dozen words since.

She sat up straight in the seat next to him, hands folded primly in her lap. At least she'd lost the schoolmarm hairstyle and clothes. And she was wearing perfume... for him. He'd noticed it when he'd helped her into the car and again when he'd kissed her.

He wondered if Kenny had called Will yet. Alex knew he would. Damn, he wished he could be there to see the look on Will's face. The revenge factor of possessing someone Will Tucker wanted felt good. And so had knowing he'd managed to anger Kenny.

A little payback on old debts.

Instead of dwelling on his victories, his thoughts wandered to other aspects of the kiss—the way Genie had melted in his arms, the sweet taste of her, the soft sigh she'd made as she'd parted her lips for him.

She was so responsive, it wasn't fair for Will to place a No Trespassing sign on her, denying her the chance for a relationship with someone else. And denying someone else the chance to experience her sensuality.

He hoped he'd set the ball rolling, and after he left town someone would get up the courage to ask her out.

But didn't she deserve a man who wouldn't have let himself be intimidated by an absent Will Tucker in the first place?

Yes, but that man is not going to be me.

"Would you like to go somewhere for coffee or a drink?" Alex asked.

"No, thanks. Tomorrow's a workday for me." The last thing Genie wanted was to prolong the evening. She wasn't sure if she wanted to cry or throw things when she got home, but she did know she wanted to be alone for whichever she chose.

The drive to her house was quiet. Alex looked preoccupied, and Genie just wanted the ordeal to be over.

Once they were parked in her driveway, Alex turned slightly to face her. "Genie, do you have a date for Grandee's birthday party?"

"No, I'm going alone."

He brought one hand up and brushed a lock of hair from her shoulder. "How about if we go together?"

"No, thanks." She slid over and started to get out of the car.

He reached out and stopped her. "You don't have a date, but you won't go with me?"

"That's right. Is it so hard for you to believe a woman might turn you down?"

"Will you at least tell me why?"

Genie took a deep breath and let it out slowly. If nothing else, at least she had her pride. "I won't pretend to know what you hoped to accomplish with the scene at the gas station, but I don't like it that you used me in your scheme. And I won't let it happen again."

Getting ready for work the next day, Genie decided to leave her hair down. If she tucked it behind her ears, it should stay out of her way.

Needing something to perk up her mood after last night's fiasco, she dug into the back of a drawer and came up with a colorful silk scarf of reds and oranges to wear with her sweater and skirt of cocoa brown. It was a small addition, but it changed the entire image of her outfit.

All day, her co-workers complimented her on how nice she looked. And all she'd done was change her hair and add some color to her outfit. What would happen if she went for a total image overhaul?

She would have to look into it.

On the way home, Genie stopped off at the local grocery store.

"You're looking fine today, Eugenia," the produce manager greeted her.

She smiled at him. "Thank you, Sam."

She moved into the next aisle. While she was comparing prices on cans of tomato sauce, two strong male arms slipped around her waist from behind.

"I agree with Sam, you are lookin' mighty fine today, Miss Eugenia," Alex said, imitating and embellishing Sam's drawl.

Genie longed to turn around, press herself against him and pull his mouth down over hers. But this time she didn't dare take what she wanted.

She supposed Alex was expecting her to try to pull away in an indignant huff. So she stood quietly, then reached out to pick up two cans. Turning, she set them in the cart.

Steeling herself against his animal magnetism, she glanced at him and said, "Next thing on the list is a package of spaghetti. It's at the end of the aisle. Shall we start out with right feet on the count of three? Or are you ready to let go of me?"

"Sam got a smile and a thank you."

"Sam meant what he said."

"And I didn't?"

"Did you?"

"Yes, I did. You look nice today." He loosened his hold and reached up to let her hair flow through his fingers. "I like your hair down."

"Thank you, Alex," she managed, politely.

"And the smile?"

"You're pushing your luck."

He laughed. "Did anyone ever tell you you're cute when you're angry?"

"No." She started pushing her cart up the aisle. Alex followed. "Did you come to the store just to annoy other customers?"

"No, Grandee sent me to buy some oatmeal so she can make me cookies."

Grandee's oatmeal cookies were well-known in Wiley. In past years they'd won at local bake-offs and the county fair and placed in the state fair.

"Oatmeal is in aisle three." Without stopping, Genie picked up a box of spaghetti and continued on.

"I'll grab it when we get there."

"We?"

"I thought I'd keep you company as you shopped."

She looked in her cart. In it were the final ingredients she needed for dinner, tomorrow's breakfast and the pot of spaghetti sauce she planned to prepare before leaving for work in the morning. Everything else on her list could wait until tomorrow after school.

She couldn't risk walking aisle by aisle with Alex. If he turned up the voltage on his charm, she would not only overlook his using her in front of Kenny, but leave herself wide open for him to do it again.

"Sorry, but I'm done." She expected him to protest or ask her to wait for him.

Instead he shrugged and said, "All right. I'll see you around then." He headed off.

Genie watched him walk away. She told herself she was grateful he'd given up so easily, but when she was totally honest she had to admit his acquiescence was annoying.

A vague hunch told her he had done it on purpose for just that reason.

* * *

Genie turned her attention to the decorations for Grandee's party, doing her best to block Alex out of her thoughts. Years of having done the same with Will helped.

But Alex made things difficult. Friday he sent flowers to school again. She expected him to arrive after class, but she didn't see him until she was heading out the front door on her way to her parents' house for the evening.

He stepped onto her front porch. "You're going out?"

"Yes. Sorry you made the trip over for nothing. You should have called first."

"Can't you cancel?"

She could call and cancel. The plans for the evening were to watch old home movies her mother had sent off and had converted to VHS. She could see them anytime.

But her pride stopped her. Alex would have to handle any gripe he had with Kenny or anyone else by himself.

She refused to let any man use her for his own purposes again.

Will had used her to help him get through college while he spent his energy on football. He'd used her to keep his apartment and fix his meals.

She'd done it, assuming once he had his career established, and they were married, there would be more of a give and take. That Will would be supportive of her career plans. Even after watching her mother fight the same battle for years, she'd optimistically thought it would be different for her.

There was no way to go back and undo the past, but she could keep from falling into the same trap again.

"No, I can't cancel."

"What time will you be back?"

He didn't seem to want to take no for an answer. "I'm not sure."

"If you get back early enough and you'd like company, call me."

Oh, sure! That made about as much sense as a mouse inviting a cat over.

She shrugged. "I don't think I'll be back very early."

"Hot date? Couldn't the guy at least have picked you up?"

"Where I'm going and who I'm going with is none of your business."

He walked toward her until she had to tilt her head to hold his gaze. "I was going to invite you over to Grandee's for oatmeal cookies."

He'd been going to take her to his great-grandmother's house? What was he up to? "Sorry." She dug her keys out of her purse, stepped around him and headed to her car.

Alex followed. "Since you helped me find the oatmeal, I thought it would be an appropriate way to say thank you."

She stopped by the driver's door. "No need to thank me."

Alex put his hands on her waist and turned her into his arms. Before she could protest, he moved his mouth down over hers.

The fire between them flared instantly, and she kissed him back, letting herself think of nothing but the wonderful sensations racing through her body.

By the time Alex pulled away, Genie didn't care about home movies, oatmeal cookies or her pride. She wanted to haul Alex into the house and upstairs to her bedroom. Actually, just making it behind the front door away from prying eyes would be sufficient for starters.

She opened her eyes slowly and looked at him.

"Like I said, call me if you get back early. Or feel free to call later, if at the end of the evening you have any unfulfilled cravings." He took a step back.

"Unfulfilled cravings?" She wished the words back as soon as she said them.

"For oatmeal cookies." He smiled. "What did you think I meant?"

Alex went to Grandee's. He was fairly certain Genie wouldn't be calling, but he didn't feel like doing any socializing.

Donny had invited him to the Dixie again, Grandee had invited him to go along with her to play bingo and his parents had called to see if he would like to go to the movies. He hadn't seen much of the film the night he'd taken Genie, but he passed anyway.

He sat down on the couch with a glass of milk and a plate of oatmeal cookies and did a little channel surfing. Nothing caught his interest.

Who are you trying to kid?

The only thing he was interested in at the moment was Genie. She looked less and less like a schoolmarm every time he saw her. But she still acted like one.

Except when he had her in his arms.

Then she was all warm, pliant, receptive female. But within seconds of the kiss ending, she was stiff and prickly again.

He would be leaving in a few days. Time was running out.

Although even if he didn't take her to bed before he left, he was sure his kisses had left a permanent impression on her.

Genie made sure she came home late. After showering and changing into her pajamas, she got into bed. Rather than sleeping, she tossed and turned, thinking about all the cravings Alex induced in her. Then she moved on to fantasize about having him fulfill them.

She did want them fulfilled. No other man had shown any interest in her since she'd moved back to Wiley. Was Alex her last chance?

But why was he pursuing her? The question still bothered her and placed an impenetrable barrier between her and her unsatisfied cravings.

She finally managed to doze off, but didn't get anywhere near enough sleep. It took several cups of coffee throughout the next day to keep her awake. Most of the morning and early afternoon, she spent gathering all the handmade items for the birthday party.

In the late afternoon, the decorating committee met at her house and helped transport everything to Roseleigh.

They arrived to find the tables and chairs set up. Zeke Conroy and a crew of men were putting the finishing touches on the bandstand at the far end of the room.

The polished wood floor glistened where the last rays of sunlight poured in through the windows. A vision of pink and red roses, flickering candlelight that seemed to grow brighter as the natural light slowly faded, and clouds of white tulle flirted at the edges of her mind.

This is no time to be dreaming about weddings, Genie. There was too much work to be done. Besides, it took two for a wedding—a bride and a groom. And there was no one even remotely resembling groom material in her life.

"Genie, where should we start?" Annabelle Foster asked.

Genie pulled out her clipboard and got everyone working.

They were halfway through their task when one of the doors to the hallway opened and Esther Dalton, Alex's grandmother, came in. Genie started to look away, but then spotted Alex entering the room. He was carrying a large box and followed Esther to a table against the far wall.

Genie went back to her work, hoping to remain unnoticed.

"Come look at this, Genie," her sister, Maggie, called.

Genie turned and saw Maggie next to Esther... and, unfortunately, Alex.

"I'll see it later. I want to get these place cards alphabetized."

Annabelle, Casey and Mrs. Hill went to see what Maggie was so excited about. Genie breathed a sigh of relief. She would go over after Alex left.

But when Alex left the table, he came straight to her. "The decorations look nice."

She kept her eyes on the place cards in front of her. "Thanks. The fresh flowers and balloons will be delivered tomorrow."

"So, how have you been?"

"Fine. And you?"

"The same. Did you have a nice time last night?"

"Yes. Did you?"

"The cookies were great."

She looked at him and wished she hadn't. He was too darned handsome for his own good... and hers. "What's all the excitement about over there?"

He tucked his hands in the back pockets of his khaki pants, drawing her glance and her thoughts to places she'd rather they not go. "Grandma made up some scrapbooks of Grandee's life."

"Sounds great. I'll have to take a peek at them when I'm done."

"When you finish for the evening, would you like to go out for coffee?"

"Sorry, I can't. My mother, sister and Annabelle rode over with me."

"I'm sure my grandmother could drop them off."

"No, thanks."

"Genie, I'd like to talk about the other night."

"I'd rather not."

He smiled. "Please?"

She fought the urge to smile back at him. It was hard to say no to his smile, even harder to resist his dimple. "As far as I'm concerned there's nothing to discuss."

"I disagree."

Genie pulled a chair out and sat down. "All right then. Let's talk."

Alex glanced at the table where the women had gathered to look through the scrapbooks. "You want to talk here?"

Genie looked, too. The women seemed completely involved in their browsing, but she caught Maggie, Annabelle, Casey and Esther stealing peeks in their direction.

She stood up, pushing the chair into place. "You've made your point. But we can't just go out for coffee. This isn't New York. By the time we're done here the only places open will be the Dixie Lounge and the bowling alley."

"I could stop by your house."

"That's what you wanted all along, isn't it? An invitation to my house." And if she was honest with herself, that was exactly what she wanted, too. But she didn't dare let it happen. "And I'll bet coffee isn't on your mind, either...except for breakfast, right? Well, let me tell you something, Mr. Dalton, I want you to keep your sexy smiles, killer dimple and toe-curling kisses away from me."

"I've got another dimple I'd be happy to show you."

She felt blood rush to her cheeks. "Just as I suspected—"

"You suspected I had a dimple on my—"

"Alex!"

He held his hands up, palms facing her. "Genie, I just want to talk. Honest."

"Fine. I'll be home around ten. You know my phone number."

Six

Genie glared at the silent phone. She didn't want to talk to Alex, but the suspense of waiting for him to call was unnerving.

Finally it rang. She breathed a sigh of relief as she picked up the receiver.

After they exchanged polite greetings, Alex said, "Angel, I'm really sorry about the other night."

"All right."

"All right?"

"All right, I accept your apology."

"You play cat and mouse with me for two days, then accept my apology in two seconds flat? Just like that, no explanations?"

"What's to explain?"

"I'll admit, I stopped at the gas station so Kenny would see us together. But I hadn't planned the kiss. When I saw how rattled he was, I acted on impulse to drive my point home."

She wasn't sure she wanted to know what his point had been, but she asked anyway. "And what was your point?"

"That you are not Will Tucker's property. That you are a free and independent woman."

"If I'm so free and independent, why did you think I needed your help? Believe me, there's not one person in this town who doesn't know Will dumped me." Her voice quivered. "The last thing they need is a reminder. I wish they'd forget the whole thing."

"Calm down, Genie. I didn't call to upset you."

"Excuse me for being upset to find out you only kissed me to prove a point to Kenny. I should have known there was no way you might be attracted to me." She left him cold when the mere sight of him sent her temperature soaring.

"Hold on, angel. You don't think I'm attracted to you? Don't forget, that wasn't the only time I kissed you. Listen, the whole thing started the night before, I ran into Kenny—"

Did she trust him to tell the truth? He'd had plenty of time to make up a convincing explanation. Even if he did tell the truth, if he had a good reason, she would be back where she'd started from.

Hopelessly in lust with a hunk who would be walking out of her life in a few days. "What good will it do to trudge back through the whole disaster?"

"I'll admit, I wasn't a complete gentleman, but a disaster? Don't you think you're exaggerating?"

"It wasn't your ego that was stomped on."

There was a pause before Alex said, "Believe me, I know how it feels to have your ego trampled. That's why I wanted to apologize. Since I have, I'll say good night."

Genie didn't have time to answer before the dial tone sounded in her ear.

Who'd stepped on Alex's ego? If she hadn't heard the pain in his voice, she would have dismissed the idea. He seemed so self-assured, so cocky. What could someone have done to hurt him?

The image of a young boy sitting alone at a table in the library or watching a game of softball from a bench on the other side of the park flashed through her mind.

Yes, Alex knew all about ego, pride and the pain others could inflict.

Once again she wished she'd been nicer to him way back when. She felt a mixture of guilt and embarrassment over the way she acted toward him.

Not that she'd done anything mean, but she hadn't paid attention to him other than when he was tutoring her. She could have at least waved or said hello when their paths had crossed.

But that would have left her open to scorn from the other kids. Would she have been strong enough to put up with the flak from them if she'd made overtures of friendship to Alex?

She'd been popular, but had she been popular enough to have gotten away with befriending an outcast and not be cast out herself? While she'd never called Alex names or teased him, standing by and letting the others get away with it had been just as bad.

Looking back, it broke her heart.

Alex hung up the phone, then went downstairs. Grandee and an assortment of family members were polishing off Grandee's oatmeal cookies. The grownups were drinking coffee; those little ones who hadn't fallen asleep were sipping milk.

In the past, Alex had always felt like an outsider at these family gatherings. Not anymore. He refused to dwell on it, but he couldn't help wondering how much happier his childhood would have been if his Georgia cousins had been more receptive to him back then.

"If you'd stayed gone another five minutes you would have missed the cookies," Donny said.

"Actually he's way ahead of all of you. Alex was here when they were coming out of the oven," Grandee said.

There was some lighthearted teasing, then the conversation turned to other subjects. The group dwindled in size, as household by household they headed for home. Alex's parents were the last to leave. They'd flown in from California and were staying with Donny's parents. Soon only Alex and Grandee remained.

"I guess we should be getting to bed, too. Tomorrow's the big day," Alex said. "Between the parade and the party, it's going to be a long one."

Grandee looked thoughtful. "I don't feel one hundred years old."

"You don't look a day over twenty-nine."

"Hogwash."

Alex laughed. "Well, you don't look one hundred, then."

Grandee sighed. "I keep waiting to feel grown up, to feel like a full-fledged adult. I'm the oldest person for miles around. Shouldn't I feel wise and mature?"

"Maybe we should hunt up some other centenarians for you to compare notes with."

"I'd rather compare notes with a good-looking eighty-year-old."

Alex laughed again.

"Speaking of lookers. I thought you said Rorke and Jesse were coming to my party." Grandee had endeared herself to Alex's two partners when he'd taken her up to New York to visit. They were flying down in the corporate jet and would arrive in the morning.

"They'll be here."

"Good. Is Rorke bringing his new wife?"

"I think so."

"His great-grandma must be so happy to have him settling down."

Alex knew what was coming. "I don't think Rorke's great-grandma is still alive."

"Well, wherever she is, I'm sure she's happy and looking forward to some great-great-grandchildren."

"Grandee, you have plenty of great-great-grandchildren. You said yourself that you couldn't keep track of all of them anymore."

"I promise I would remember the names of yours. Little great-great-grandsons that look just like your great-grandpa." She sighed again.

He could picture them.

But he could also picture little girls with dark hair in ringlets and pretty hazel eyes, looking the way Genie had years ago when he'd first seen her perched on a stool behind the counter of her father's hardware store.

Cute little girls who would grow into teenagers driving the young men wild in their skimpy cheerleading skirts and tight sweaters. Who would send burgeoning male hormones into overdrive, the way the sight of Genie decked out for cheerleading practice had sent his.

Genie. Why did his thoughts always drift back to Genie?

This evening at Roseleigh, he'd wanted to sweep her up in his arms and carry her off to someplace secluded. There was a spark and a fire in her the last few days that hadn't been there when he'd arrived. A spark and a fire he found alluring.

But the wounded look in her eyes had stopped him.

Why should he care?

She hadn't cared about his feelings all those years ago. Besides, his motive the other evening had been to

get the word out that she no longer wore a Reserved for
Will Tucker sign. His target had been Will. But Genie
had gotten caught in the cross fire.

He wanted to leave her hot and bothered, aware of
what she'd passed up so long ago, but he hadn't
planned to hurt her feelings.

"Grandee, I'll probably get married one of these
days. And I'll name my first daughter after you, how's
that?"

"I just hope I'm around to hold her."

He put his arm around his great-grandmother's
shoulder and rested his head next to hers. "I hope you
are, too."

Genie was still feeling a bit guilty when she woke up
the next morning. She took extra care with her appearance, thinking she might run into Alex. She supposed it was her turn to apologize.

When she was ready, she headed for her parents'
house. They were going to have breakfast, go to church
and then watch the parade from in front of her father's hardware store.

It was a great location, right across the street from
the VIP's viewing stand. And there would be large
numbers of media photographers and camerapersons
recording the event.

After briefly wondering where Alex would be
watching the parade, Genie pushed thoughts of him to
the back of her mind. She bought bags of popcorn for

her nephews, waved to students past and present and managed to get into the spirit of the event.

The Boy Scout honor guard was the first down the route. The roar of the crowd worked its way along the street like a wave, almost, but not quite, drowning out the growl of a motorcycle engine.

There was more than one motorcycle in town, but Genie knew instinctively that when the bike came into sight Alex would be on it. She was right.

The sight of him in black leather pants and black leather jacket sent her senses into a tailspin. He looked good enough to cheer for, but Genie was sure most of the enthusiasm was for the petite black-leather-clad figure sitting behind him waving and blowing kisses to the crowd. Grandee.

Alex stopped the bike in front of the viewing stand. Sheriff Zeke Conroy helped Grandee off the bike, then led her to her seat. After a short speech by Wiley's mayor, Grandee was given the key to the city and the parade began again.

Genie kept half her attention on the entries but the rest kept shifting to Alex, who was now seated in the grandstand.

There was plenty of clapping and calling out greetings to familiar faces making their way past, but then the overwhelming roar that had greeted Grandee started again. Since Grandee was already in her seat, who was causing the commotion? Genie raised up on tiptoes and tried to catch a glimpse through the moving crowd

The question was answered when she heard some-one call out, "Willy Boy, hey, Willy!"

Will was here?

The photographers and newscasters surged for-ward. When the car finally came into her view, Genie glanced briefly at Will, then looked at his companion. One of the team cheerleaders.

The two of them posed and smiled for the cameras and waved to the crowd. It was bad enough seeing him on television. Having him only yards away with an-other woman tucked close against him was more than she could stand.

She carefully worked her way to the back row on the sidewalk, then slipped between buildings to the next block.

Escaping.

Alex had spotted Genie in the crowd across the street as soon as he'd taken his seat in the grandstand. Watching her, he'd felt a familiar tightening in his loins.

The ordinary schoolmarm had blossomed into a stunning brunette over the last few days. Now more than before he was dying to have her in the sheets with him.

Cheers and screams pulled his attention to the fes-tivities. From where he sat above the crowds, he had a clear view of the convertible making its way down Main Street.

It had been years since he'd seen him, but he recognized Will Tucker right away. After a quick glance at the blonde by Will's side, Alex sought out Genie in the crowd. He knew the moment she spotted Will.

All the sparkle seemed to go out of her.

Without a word to anyone, she turned and headed through the crowd. Alex didn't stop to think, just told his father to tell Grandee he would see her at the house and started after Genie.

Once at street level, he wove between a troop of Girl Scouts dressed as flowers and the Wiley high school band to reach the other side. By the time he made his way through the spectators on the sidewalk and followed Genie's route onto the next block, she was nowhere in sight.

Genie's sobs slowed to ragged sniffles. She knelt next to the cedar chest at the foot of her bed. Embroidered linens and quilts were pushed to one side so she could unfold the white wedding dress carefully packed away beneath.

After unfolding the fragile tissue paper, she ran her hands lovingly over the dress. Taking it with her, she slowly got up, slipped off her shoes, then curled up in the middle of the bed, snuggling into the throw pillows.

She heard the doorbell ring but closed her eyes, as if that would somehow make whoever it was go away. Of course she knew it was Maggie, and Maggie wouldn't be put off simply because Genie didn't answer the door.

Right on cue, Genie heard knocking, a pause, then the sound of the front door opening. Maggie was coming up the staircase more slowly than usual.

Genie sat up and wiped at the last of her tears as the sound of footsteps neared her bedroom. "I know what you're going to say, and ... Alex!"

Genie got off the bed, leaving the dress. "I thought you were Maggie. Sorry I didn't answer the door. I ... I ..." He looked so large and masculine standing in her room. The black leather pants and jacket he wore fit like a second skin.

"Are you all right?"

"I'm fine." She tried to smile, but her bottom lip wouldn't stop quivering.

Alex came to stand in front of her. "Ah, hell, angel, do you still love him that much?"

"Yes ..." But if she loved Will, would she be longing to run her hands over Alex? "No..." But then why had the sight of Will with that woman sent her running for home? "I don't know." The waterworks started again.

Alex took her into his arms, rocking her gently.

When she saw a teardrop roll down the leather of his jacket, she pulled back. "I don't want to get your jacket wet."

He pulled down the double zippers, shrugged out of his jacket and tossed it onto the easy chair in the corner. The T-shirt he wore rippled with each movement.

Easy, Genie, he's just taking off his jacket.

It was *just* his jacket, but he was taking it off in her bedroom!

She couldn't help wondering if his leather pants would make the same creaking sound slipping down his legs as the jacket was making.

Once he held her again, the last thing she felt like doing was crying. The heat of his body warmed her cheek through the stretchy fabric. She snuggled closer, breathing in the scent of his after-shave, basking in the comfort of strong masculine arms around her.

He moved his hands over her back in soothing circular motions. If she could only stay here forever.

"I take it you didn't know Will was going to be here."

"No." Her voice was muffled against his chest.

Alex slid one of his hands all the way up beneath her hair to settle on the bare, sensitive skin on the back of her neck. A shiver raced down her spine, moving her against his rock-hard length. Her breath caught in her throat, then escaped with a sound between a moan and a whimper.

The pressure on her neck increased, urging her to look up, but her muscles refused to move. Alex brought his other hand up, cupping it beneath her chin, tilting her head back.

"He's not the only man in the world."

"I know."

"Then give someone else a chance."

"You?"

"That'll work." He moved his mouth down onto hers.

The hardwood floor seemed to tilt beneath her feet. She grasped at his shoulders, hoping to steady herself. Her hands tingled from the warmth beneath. Slowly she unclenched them and traced across the hard planes of his chest.

The kiss grew. Urgent and hungry, a duel they were both winning.

Impatient with the fabric covering him, Genie slipped her hands down to work his T-shirt out of his waistband. Once it was free, she nudged under the hem and felt his heat directly. Crisp hair curled around her fingers and tickled her palms as she moved her hands upward.

Alex growled against her mouth and took the liberty of mirroring her motions until his hands lay against her bare skin, as well.

She had never felt anything like it. His touch was gentle, almost reverent as he slowly feathered his way up until he reached the lace barrier of her bra.

He ended the kiss, pulling back to look at her, holding her gaze as he moved his fingers up to tease her nipples into tight nubs. This time, she was the one to follow his lead, feeling his body respond in a similar manner. She sighed and went up on tiptoe to reclaim his mouth.

The kiss was brief, then Alex moved to give himself room to pull off her sweatshirt. His shirt and her bra followed.

He leaned back and looked at her. "Beautiful," he murmured, bringing his hands up to cover her breasts again.

She could have said the same about him, if she'd had the breath to speak.

The tanned width of his chest was sprinkled with golden hair that darkened as the trail led lower to swirl around his navel and disappear beneath black leather. As her gaze continued down, she saw clear evidence that Alex wanted her.

A dart of pleasure shot through her. But whether it was from knowing he wanted her or because he'd moved one hand down to trace the path of her zipper, she wasn't sure.

She moaned and Alex caught the sound with his lips. He swept her into his arms and headed for the bed. He laid her down gently, but didn't follow.

"What the..." He reached down and picked up the wedding dress she'd abandoned.

Genie sat up and took it from him, using it to cover her bare breasts. "I bought it when I was engaged to Will."

His eyes were narrowed, his mouth a tight line, and his chest rose and fell with the ragged rhythm of arrested arousal. "You came that close to being married?"

She nodded. "Everything was planned down to the last rose petal."

Alex continued staring at the dress.

In an attempt to fill the awkward silence, Genie continued, "We were going to be married at Rose-leigh...at sunset...." Her words made the scene vivid in her mind. "In the ballroom, with pink and red roses and candles and white lace tablecloths." With one hand, she smoothed the skirt of the dress. "I'd dreamed of being married there since I was a little girl."

With a last deep breath and whoosh of released air, Alex moved his gaze to hers. "Shouldn't who you're marrying be the most important detail?"

"I decided I wanted to marry Will when I was twelve." She ran her hand over the lace appliqué on the dress's bodice. The stiff fabric shifted, rubbing across her tight nipples, reminding her she was half naked.

She looked at Alex, startled once again by the sharp stab of hungry desire the sight of him sparked. But when she looked into his eyes, she knew her chances of having the hunger satisfied were gone.

She went over and picked up her sweatshirt. With her back to him, she dropped the dress to the floor and, without bothering with her bra, slipped the shirt on.

She turned to face him. "It was thoughtful of you to check on me. Thank you."

"Anytime." He stood and walked over to gather up his T-shirt and jacket. "You okay now?"

"Fine." It was a bold-faced lie.

"I'll see you this evening then."

"This evening?"

"Grandee's party."

Will would probably be there. "I won't be going."

"You can't miss Grandee's birthday party."

"I don't think I could stand to be there alone, watching the two of them together."

"Well, then, would you reconsider my offer to go with me?"

Seven

————

She could go to the party with the downright gorgeous CEO of Yankee Motorworks. "I don't know, Alex. I didn't appreciate it when you used me in your plot against Kenny. It hardly seems fair for me to turn around and use you to get back at Will."

"But there's a big difference. I'm asking you to let me help you with this."

He did have a point. "I'm just not sure."

"Please?"

Will had always been her vision of the ultimate male, but as she looked at Alex, she had to admit she found him more appealing. "You make it hard to say no."

"Then say yes."

She shrugged her shoulders in resignation, hoping she wasn't making a mistake. "All right. I'll go to Grandee's party with you."

"I'll pick you up at six-thirty."

"All right."

He nodded, then turned to go.

The sight of his bare back and the black leather hugging his rear was almost too much for her to let get away...again.

Genie bit down on her bottom lip to keep from calling to him. Instead, she listened to the sound of him going down the stairs. He paused in the living room and she hoped he might change his mind. Then she heard the sound of a zipper and realized he must be dressing.

Moments later she heard the front door open and close.

Alex walked to Grandee's house. He would pick up the motorcycle from the grandstand later. He didn't feel like answering questions about where he'd gone.

Besides, he needed to lie down. He felt like he'd run a marathon.

Thoughts of lying down brought visions of Genie's bed. He'd come so close to being in it with her. A vision of her smooth skin coming into view inch by inch as he'd pulled her sweatshirt off flashed into his mind.

He'd guessed right, she had been hiding a beautiful body beneath all the baggy clothes. A responsive body.

She'd been ready and willing . . . then he'd found that dress.

Damn the bad luck!

He wanted to make love to the self-righteous prom queen who had thought she and her friends were too good for him.

He had no desire to take advantage of the emotional turmoil of a jilted woman crying over a girlhood dream wedding.

Maggie called Genie from their parents' house after the parade. "Genie, are you all right?"

"Yes."

"Are you alone?"

"Yes, I'm alone. Why?"

"I had just told Jackson to watch the kids and I was about to follow you when I saw Alex leave the parade. I thought he was going to your house."

"He was here."

"And?"

"And he's coming back this evening to pick me up for Grandee's party."

"Good deal!"

Alex's gaze swept over her, reminding Genie he'd seen or touched most of what her dress covered.

"Beautiful." He said it in the same tone he'd used this afternoon.

Her breasts tingled at the memory. Genie was glad she'd changed from what she'd originally planned to wear to the party.

She'd dug into the back of her closet and come up with a seductive little number she'd bought to wear to a dinner with Will that she'd ended up not attending. Hanging in the front of her closet with her current wardrobe, it had stood out like a bird of paradise in a chicken coop.

"You look nice, too." He was wearing a suit and tie and looked every inch the big-time executive. He looked sophisticated, but sexy. The sight of him bare-chested flashed into her thoughts.

"Are you ready to go?"

I'd rather go upstairs to the bedroom. "Yes." She followed him out, locking the door behind her. "A limousine?"

Alex shrugged. "Rorke and Jesse showed up with it."

"Rorke and Jesse?"

"The other two owners of Yankee. They're big fans of Grandee and came down for the celebration."

She'd ridden in a limousine with Will before, but that seemed like another lifetime. This morning seemed like another lifetime, too.

"Nervous?" Alex asked.

"About meeting your partners? Do they bite?"

"I mean about seeing Will."

Since Alex seemed comfortable with being a buffer between her and Will, she allowed herself to let go of any notion that she was using him. "I think I can handle it. I've had a few hours to get used to the idea." Knowing she looked her best helped, too.

Once in the limo, Alex introduced Genie to Jesse Tyler, Rorke O'Neil and Rorke's wife, Callie.

Whoever coined the phrase tall, dark and handsome must've had Alex's partners in mind. Jesse's hair was dark brown and his eyes a clear shade of emerald green. Rorke's hair was black and his eyes were blue. Callie was a classically beautiful blonde. She reminded Genie of a young Grace Kelly.

On the way out of town, Alex gave his friends the fifty-cent rundown on the passing sights.

"It seems like a nice little town," Callie said. "It's about the same size as Harrison, Vermont, where Rorke and I live," she told Genie.

"Oh, I assumed you all lived in New York."

Alex answered. "We used to, but as the company has grown we've spread out. Rorke moved up to our new Vermont plant and Jesse alternates between New York, central Florida and Arizona."

"While we're on the subject of Yankee, Mike Maxwell has started calling again, Alex," Jesse said.

"I got his messages. I'll call him when I get back tomorrow."

Tomorrow.

Alex would be leaving so soon? This would be her last night with him.

Her newly reawakened sexual needs sent up a loud protest. She knew in the long nights ahead she would lie awake wondering what it would have been like to make love with him. Unless he stayed with her tonight.

"Why don't you just give him an interview and get it over with?" Rorke said.

"I offered him an interview, but he wants the interview and an exclusive on the identity of the models."

Jesse swore, then apologized to the ladies.

Genie thought back to the evening Alex had offered to let her bribe the information out of him. She should have jumped at the chance. If only she'd known then how his kisses affected her. "Are you planning to reveal their identities?"

Alex shook his head. "And give up all the free publicity?"

"Publicity is great, but is there any solid indication whether the campaign is helping sales yet?" Rorke asked.

"The third quarter report should be done soon. But even if sales haven't been boosted, the whole thing has been great at building us stronger name recognition."

"Enough shop talk, guys," Callie said. "Genie, how long have you lived in Wiley?"

The rest of the ride to Roseleigh was pleasant. The conversation and banter kept Genie's mind off Will until the limo pulled up to the front steps. She wondered if he was already here.

Will disappeared from her thoughts again when Alex took her hand to help her step out of the car. Images from this afternoon rose up to haunt her, sending her pulse racing.

She looked into Alex's eyes.

He smiled.

Could he tell what she was thinking? She felt her cheeks grow warm.

His smile widened. He knew, all right.

If it hadn't been for the wedding dress, she and Alex would have made love this afternoon.

Once again Will had stolen something from her—it might not be as far-reaching as the way he'd kept her from her hopes and dreams of a loving family, but then again maybe it was.

Alex's kisses were so magical, and the way she'd felt when his hands had roamed over her bare skin... maybe not being able to make love with him was disrupting her future.

Genie wasn't about to let Will spoil the rest of this evening.

She smiled at Alex. He tucked her arm around his and led the way into the house.

''Hey, this is almost as big as your place, Rorke,'' Jesse said as they stepped into the entryway.

Callie laughed.

Genie envied the casual way the other woman linked her arm with her husband's and the potent force of love written on both their faces whenever they looked at each other.

To put the thoughts out of her mind, Genie wondered about Alex's home. Where he spent his days, and his nights . . . and how often he wasn't alone.

There were a number of people milling around the ballroom when they got there. They stopped to say happy birthday to Grandee before finding their table.

It wasn't until after dinner and the blowing out of the birthday candles that Genie thought to look for Will. He was several tables over, sitting next to Skip Evans, and he was watching her.

Surprisingly, she didn't feel anything. Even the sight of the blonde by his side didn't bother her this evening. Amazing, when up until recently she'd been sure he was the love of her life.

Esther Dalton enlisted Alex, Rorke and Jesse to help move Grandee's gifts from the gift table to the head table so she could open them. Callie turned her chair so she could have a better view.

With everyone's attention elsewhere, Will slipped into the chair next to Genie.

"How have you been, Genie?"

She smiled politely. "Fine, and you?"

He shrugged. "Can't complain."

"Good."

He put his arm around the back of her chair and leaned closer to her, lowering his voice. "Watch your step with Alex Dalton."

"Excuse me?"

"I think he's using you to get back at me."

Genie laughed. "What does he have against you?"

"You know we were never friends."

"You don't try to get back at someone just because he wasn't your friend."

"It's a little more than that. The summer he was helping you with summer school, the guys and I surprised him in the woods one day. He was practicing to ask you out."

Alex had been practicing to ask her out? He'd never given any indication that he had any interest in her back then. In fact, when her mother had invited him to her party, he hadn't shown up. She'd been relieved at the time. But if he'd really been practicing to ask her out, wouldn't he have jumped at the chance to be at her party? "He never asked me out."

"Of course not. By the time the guys and I got through with him, he wouldn't have dared."

A sick feeling started in her stomach. Could this be what was behind Alex's strange behavior at the gas station? "Was Kenny there?"

"More than likely. I don't remember for sure."

Even if Kenny hadn't been there, Alex would assume Kenny would pass word on to Will about their visit. "Thanks for the advice, Will, but maybe Alex asked me out because he's interested in me. He wanted to before. Maybe he figured since you were out of the picture he could."

But then why had he made sure to kiss her in front of Kenny? She wondered if Alex's insistence on her coming to the party with him tonight had been for his own purposes, too, and not to help her through the evening, as he'd implied.

"Revenge is a powerful motivator, Genie. Look at him. Do you think he's so desperate for dates that he has to go back and hunt up country girls he used to have a crush on?"

Genie looked to the front of the room where Alex was standing. The man had more than his allotment of sex appeal, that was for sure.

She glanced at the other tables. Many of the women were watching Alex, although Rorke and Jesse were getting their share of attention, too. The answer to Will's question was obvious. "Even if he is motivated by revenge, what difference does it make to you?"

"I don't want to see you hurt. He's using you, baby."

Genie laughed. "It's all right for you to use me, but not anyone else?"

Will's eyes narrowed and the muscles along his jaw tightened. "Look, I'm trying to save—"

Genie stood up and pushed her chair in. "Thanks for the advice, but mind your own business."

Will started to open his mouth, but Genie turned and headed for the ladies' room.

Genie stepped into the hallway and started back to the party. A movement near the window caught her eye. She was afraid it was Will. Relief swept over her when she saw it was Alex.

She smiled as he walked over to her.

What difference did it make why Alex had asked her out—revenge, the fulfillment of an old crush, an offer of friendship or merely acting on the desire that flared between them?

"I saw you talking to Will. Is everything okay?" Alex asked.

"Just fine."

He reached out and took her into his arms. "I'm glad. You know you deserve better. You'll find someone else to wear that wedding dress for. And when you do, you'll realize he was worth the wait."

Only if he kisses me the way you do. What were the chances of that? "This afternoon you asked for a chance."

"Whoa, angel, we were talking about something completely different at that point."

"Were we?"

"I was."

"Maybe I'm interested in what you were offering." She pressed her body to his and kissed him.

He returned the kiss. Slowly he backed them up until Genie felt the wall behind her. Then he moved closer.

Genie gasped when she recognized how aroused he was. He wanted her. There was no denying it. It couldn't be strictly a revenge thing, as Will had implied.

Alex moved his mouth off hers, placing soft kisses along her jaw, then against the side of her neck. "Did I tell you how great you look in that dress?"

"Do you think so?"

His answer was a muffled growl against her neck.

She kissed his temple and tried to work her way over to his mouth, but he gently pulled away. "Sorry, angel. But I think we'd better get back to the party. There are too many bedrooms around, and I'm running short on willpower."

Grandee was still opening gifts when they got back to the party, but she was on the last batch and Rorke and Jesse had returned to the table. Genie's glass was empty, and there wasn't a waiter in sight. So after seating her, Alex went to get Genie a refill.

As he started back, Donny waved him over.

"Genie looks like a whole new woman, Alex. Everyone's talking about it. And Will's watching the two of you like a hawk."

Alex shrugged. He couldn't blame Will or any other man for staring. Genie looked terrific tonight. He would like nothing more than to disappear into one of the bedroom suites with her and not come out until morning.

But he couldn't shake the vision of her tear-filled eyes looking at him as she clutched her unworn wedding dress to her bared breasts.

Donny continued, "At first I thought you were nuts for wanting to go out with her, but I must admit you've got a good eye."

Alex squeezed Donny's shoulder. "Thanks." He knew his cousin meant it as high praise, but it really torqued his gears that physical appearance was still so important to the men in this town.

Like you're any different?

But he was . . . he'd been on both sides of the fence.

Shortly after Alex left, Maggie slipped into the seat next to Genie. Genie introduced her to Jesse, Rorke and Callie.

Maggie lowered her voice so only Genie could hear. "So, how's it going?"

"Fine."

Maggie smiled. "You're here with one of the most gorgeous men on the planet and everything is fine?"

Genie nodded. "Yes."

"You look great. That's a killer dress."

"Thanks."

"Dad didn't recognize you at first."

Genie fought to keep from laughing. "Really?"

"And he's not the only one. Lots of people were wondering who the woman with Alex was until Kenny realized it was you and started spreading the word around."

"Good ol' Kenny."

"I saw Will sneak over to talk to you. I would have come over, but it looked like you had everything under control."

"I did."

Maggie gave her a quick hug. "I'm proud of you, Genie. I was really worried when you ran off during the parade."

Alex came back and Maggie excused herself.

Grandee was finally finished with her presents and the band started playing. Alex asked her to dance. He held her close through several songs, then took his place in line to dance with the birthday girl.

Genie saw Will heading in her direction, but when he asked her to dance she felt a hand on her elbow and a cool, masculine voice said, "I believe this dance is mine."

Genie looked behind her to see Jesse. "Yes, I think you're right. Sorry, Will."

"No problem."

Jesse took her hand and led her onto the dance floor.

"Thank you for rescuing me."

He smiled at her. "Glad to be of service."

He was a good dancer, and he kept a respectable distance between them.

"Alex said you and Rorke designed the motorcycle that started Yankee Motorworks."

"Yes, but having a good product is only a small part of the success of a company. I don't know what we would have done without Alex. He's got a great mind for business, although it did take quite a bit of coaxing to get him to lose the pocket protector."

"Didn't he meet you when he was in graduate school?"

"Yes."

"And he still had his pocket protector?"

"Yes."

Genie had assumed Alex's metamorphosis had taken place much earlier, closer to the time she'd seen him last. But apparently not.

Jesse asked, "Have you known him long?"

"He visited Grandee every summer, but I didn't really meet him until his last summer here when he tutored me in algebra."

"Speaking of Alex..."

Genie turned to follow Jesse's gaze and found Alex right behind her. "Mind if I cut in?"

The rest of the evening passed quickly, and before Genie knew it, they were getting ready to leave. Grandee rode back to town with them, sitting next to Alex, holding his hand. As the car started down the driveway she yawned.

"Did you have a good time?" Alex asked his great-grandmother.

"Yes. But such a big fuss, Alex. Don't do this much next year." Her voice faded away and her eyes closed.

"Not until your two hundredth birthday, I promise."

Alex leaned down and kissed the top of Grandee's head.

Genie felt a strange lump form in her throat. This was the tender side of Alex she'd glimpsed briefly today when he'd comforted her. Surely a man capable of tenderness was capable of love, marriage and commitment.

Of course maybe Alex's insistence that he wasn't interested in anything more than an affair might only apply to her. Maybe he was interested in getting married, but she wasn't the one he wanted.

Well, she hadn't been the one Will had wanted, either. She'd spent years being unhappy about it. She refused to make the same mistake over Alex.

The conversation in the car was quieter, but no less lively than on the drive out. Genie liked Alex's friends and was glad he had such nice people in his life.

The driver stopped at her house first, canceling any chance of her asking Alex to come in. After she said goodbye to the others, Alex walked her to the door.

"Thank you for the lovely evening," she said.

"My pleasure." He leaned down and kissed her.

She could taste the goodbye.

"Take care, angel."

Genie threw herself heart and soul into her work. Between her job and her family, she was able to keep all the hours of the day full. It was only the long hours at night when thoughts of Alex would torment her.

Especially thoughts about the way it had felt to be half naked in his arms—smooth feminine breast pressed against hair-roughened masculine muscle. In the moonlit dimness of her room, she could almost see him standing in her doorway.

She tried to discuss the problem with Maggie, but her sister's response had been to try her hand at matchmaking Genie with some of her husband's friends from a neighboring town.

The men were nice, but none of them sent her pulses racing.

"Maybe you'll have to lower your standards," Maggie told her. "Will and Alex are tough acts to follow. It's not fair to compare these guys to them."

"I'm not." *At least not on a conscious level.*

"Jackson has another cousin—"

"No more blind dates. It makes me seem so desperate."

"You were the first girl in your high school class to get engaged, Genie. And you're the only one who hasn't been married at least once."

"Thanks for the reminder, Sis."

"So, should I set something up for Saturday night?"

"No. It's time we face the fact that I might never get married."

"Is that what you want?"

"It's not what I want, but I think it's what I need to settle for."

When the opportunity to get away from Wiley for a few days came, Genie jumped at the chance. One of the teachers had been scheduled to attend a computer seminar in Boston, but when a family crisis arose, Genie was offered the trip.

By taking an extra two days off work, plus the four-day Thanksgiving weekend, she could have a nice long break. She'd never been to Boston, and there was a lot of history she would like to see. It was also much closer to New York City than Wiley was.

Alex opened the door to his apartment.

"Help yourself to a drink," he told Jesse. "I'll be right down." He climbed the stairs and headed for the master bedroom to change into casual clothing. They were heading to a party given by an artist friend Jesse dated off and on when he was in town. Alex was hoping to meet someone new and exciting to bring home with him.

Since getting back from Wiley, he'd flipped through his phone book several times. Most of the women listed would jump at the chance to go out with him again, but for some reason, he couldn't work up enough enthusiasm to ask out any of the gorgeous, sexy women he'd dated.

He couldn't get the vision of Genie the last night he'd seen her out of his mind. Genie, looking like a grown-up version of the beautiful teenager she'd been.

Once he was downstairs, he stopped by his home office and checked for phone messages. He made a few notes on a legal pad until the next voice made his hand stop, pen poised in mid-stroke.

"Alex, it's Genie Hill. I'll be going up to Boston next week and thought I'd stop off in New York to do some shopping on my way home. If you've got some spare time, maybe we could get together. Give me a call."

"I was wondering which one of you would break down first."

Alex turned to see Jesse leaning casually against the door frame.

Jesse continued, "You must have knocked her sweet Georgia socks off, Dalton."

"I didn't get the chance."

"Sounds like the chance can be yours if you want it. And if you don't, I'll take her number."

He shot Jesse a dirty look.

Jesse shrugged, then turned and headed to the living room. Alex reached down and picked up the phone.

Eight

Genie was finishing up dinner dishes when the phone rang.

"Hello."

"Hi, angel. I got your message."

A thrill of excitement shot through her. "Alex."

"When will you be in New York?"

"I'll be arriving either late Tuesday or early Wednesday. I'll know more after I talk to a travel agent and line up flight and hotel reservations."

"You could stay with me."

She wanted to see him, but did she want the total temptation of sleeping under the same roof? "I wouldn't want to impose."

"I wouldn't offer if it was an imposition."

"I'll be in town through Sunday. What about your plans for Thanksgiving?"

"I've been invited to a friend's for dinner, but the invitation was for two. You can join me if you'd like."

"If you're sure..."

"Positive."

"All right then."

"Just one thing."

"Yes?"

"You're welcome to the guest room. But I think I should warn you, I plan to do my best to convince you to join me in mine."

"I..."

"Do you want to change your mind and stay at a hotel?"

Genie took a deep breath and let it out slowly. "No. I want to stay with you."

"I'll be counting the days."

Genie didn't realize how much she'd missed Alex until she stepped out of the jetway and saw him waiting, a bouquet of flowers in his hand.

She wasn't sure how she should greet him. They both knew there was a strong possibility they would become lovers sometime in the next few days.

When she got closer, it seemed natural to step into his arms.

"Hi, angel."

"Alex."

He leaned forward and kissed her briefly but skill-fully. Any lingering doubts disappeared. She was glad she'd come.

Her haircut was new, along with the fashionable pantsuit she was wearing and the new clothes in her garment bag. She'd spent her spare time in Boston on a makeover and shopping trip.

She felt like a whole new woman.

The woman she would have been today if she hadn't gone so far to pieces over Will.

"Do you have any other luggage?" Alex asked.

"No, this is it."

"Shall we go then?"

After the luxurious ride to Roseleigh, Genie had ex-pected a limo or a luxury car and was surprised when Alex led her to a sleek red Ferrari. But as she watched him maneuver the car through afternoon traffic, she realized how perfectly the car fit him.

The upper east side apartment building where he lived was large and had a doorman who greeted him by name. The lobby was spacious and elegant. Genie pic-tured Alex striding across the marble tiles on his way to work each morning.

He stood close to her in the elevator. Closer than necessary to accommodate the other people sharing the space with them.

Once they entered his apartment, Genie tried not to stare. There was a professional look to the decor, and the view was awe-inspiring.

"It's lovely, Alex."

"Thanks. Would you like the fifty-cent tour or would you like to freshen up?"

She reached her hand up to smooth her hair. It would have to wait. She wasn't ready to be away from Alex. "Tour, please."

In the modern kitchen, he helped her fill a vase with water for her flowers, which they left on the glass table in the breakfast nook.

Despite what he'd said on the phone, when he showed her the guest room he left her luggage at the foot of the bed before continuing on.

They ended in the master bedroom suite. Upstairs, it offered the same wonderful view as the living room. Genie concentrated on the view, trying to ignore the king-size bed.

"So," Alex said. "What would you like to see? The Empire State Building, Statue of Liberty, Central Park, a museum?"

You, without your clothes. All of them this time.

But she wasn't that bold . . . yet. "Whatever is easiest. This is my first time in the city, so everything will be new."

He walked over to stand in front of her. Reaching out, he placed his hands on either side of her neck, tilting her chin with his thumbs. "You're going to leave the agenda to me?"

Was he talking about sight-seeing or something else? Either way, her answer was the same. "Yes."

"All right, I'll make sure you have a weekend to remember." He ran one thumb across her lower lip before reaching down to take her hand.

There was a limo waiting downstairs when they stepped out of the building. Genie had looked forward to seeing the sights of New York, but found most of her attention focused on Alex. His smile, his blue eyes, his golden hair, his gorgeous body now hidden inside his oh-so-civilized power suit.

All around them were the hustle and bustle of the big city, yet she felt some invisible barrier cocooning her and Alex from the rest of the world. Even the driver, on the other side of the glass, seemed detached.

Alex sat close to her on the spacious leather seat. One arm stretched behind her back, the other rested on his leg. Genie fought back the urge to set her hand on his other leg.

They took a driving tour of well-known landmarks, most of which Genie had seen in movies, on television or on postcards. Alex filled her in on history and architectural information.

"You certainly know a lot about the city."

"I've picked it up the last few years."

"I'm curious, what made you decide on New York for your headquarters?"

"Our major investor was the Westbrook Foundation. They wanted to keep a close eye on us at first, so they moved our headquarters into their building."

When they rode down Broadway, Alex said, "We've got tickets for the theater Saturday night."

"Listen, don't feel obligated to entertain me *all* weekend. If you already have other plans, I'm sure I can keep myself busy."

"I want to entertain you." His gaze dropped to her lips. "Hungry?" he asked.

Oh, yes! She had to bite her tongue to keep from saying the words out loud. Alex was talking about food. "A little. Are you?"

He looked up and smiled. "Ravenous."

Now she wasn't so sure he meant food, after all.

The restaurant he took her to was upscale, the food delicious and the company wonderful, but Genie couldn't eat much. After dinner, they went into the bar and listened to the jazz band finish its set.

They sat close together in the booth, as they had earlier in the car. Genie felt surprisingly at ease and comfortable. She'd expected to be nervous. Maybe Alex had a soothing effect on her. Or maybe the mellow notes of the saxophone were draining the stress away as they flowed over her.

She wished the club had a dance floor; she wanted to be held in Alex's arms.

Instead, aware of the warmth of him pressed against her side, she leaned her head against his shoulder.

"Tired, angel?"

She turned her head and looked at him. He was so close it would only take a slight movement to touch his mouth with her own. "No. Just very comfortable."

He reached both arms around her, locking his fingers together against her waist. "This is comfortable, but wouldn't it be even better curled up together on my couch? Think how good it would feel—" he placed a soft kiss on her lips "—for us to get out of... our shoes."

As she was sure he intended, his words created a vivid image of the two of them getting out of much more than their shoes. "All right."

In the back seat of the limo, Genie turned to Alex. The polite thank you for a lovely time she'd planned to offer never materialized.

The sight of him in the dim glow from the lights on the street beyond took her breath away. And when he turned and looked at her, his eyes were lit with burning passion.

Her heartbeat accelerated. All her protective instincts told her she was playing a dangerous game. She'd thought through her decision to come to New York before calling Alex in the first place. But she wished she'd thought it through more carefully—considered the danger.

Alex was the first man she'd felt a powerful attraction to, other than Will. Add to that her finally getting over Will, and Alex's charming ways, and she was in real danger of falling head over heels in love with him.

But at the moment, what she wanted most was to be swept into his arms, held tightly against him and kissed until she forgot her own name.

As if he could read her mind, Alex reached out and brought her to him, moving his mouth over hers, sliding his tongue across her lips until she parted them and let him in. She sighed when he curved his hands around her sensitive breasts and teased her nipples through the soft silk of her blouse.

He tasted of coffee and warm male. She leaned in to him, wrapping her arms around his neck, tangling her fingers through the soft hair on the back of his head.

Alex reached down, turned her toward him and lifted her until she straddled him. Uncomfortable at first, she started to pull away, but his hands held her in place until she yielded to the erotic feel of his body and relaxed against him.

She couldn't miss the extent of his arousal. Deep within her was an answering throbbing need. They were pressed so tightly together, surely he could feel it. But no, he would have to be inside, at the source of her need, before he would know.

And that was exactly where she wanted him.

She wanted to tell him, but he was still kissing her, and she wanted that even more. His hands curved around her breasts again. Then with a frustrated groan, he pulled his mouth from hers and slid down to tease the peak with his tongue, right through the silk and the lace beneath.

When she thought she couldn't take any more, he stopped the teasing and sent her farther into rhapsody by sucking gently. After long delectable moments, he moved his mouth back to hers. When he ended the kiss, she tried to pull him to her.

He resisted. "Soon, angel."

He moved her to sit by his side. Pulling the lapels of her jacket together, he hid the telltale wetness as Genie felt the car come to a smooth stop. She ran her fingers through her hair, doing what she could without the help of a brush or mirror.

The doorman helped her out of the limo and Alex guided her into the building to the elevators.

Two young, attractive women got into the elevator with them. Both greeted Alex by name.

Genie was extremely aware of the swollen feel of her lips and the wetness hidden behind her jacket.

She was also aware of the women studying her covertly. She wondered if Alex had gone out with either of the women...or both. She knew so little about his life, his relationships.

She looked at his profile, remembering the way he'd looked years ago. She should have realized back then that his strong jaw and high cheekbones were more important than the condition of his skin or the horn-rimmed glasses that kept slipping down his nose.

He turned, catching her watching him. He winked.

"Alex," one of the women said, "we saw you on TV the other day. At your grandma's birthday."

"My great-grandmother."

"She looked so cute riding behind you."

Genie wondered if either of the women had ridden with Alex.

The other woman spoke up. "Was that really her first motorcycle ride? Or was that just a publicity thing?"

"That was her first," Alex said.

"They showed clips of Will Tucker, too. Did you have a chance to meet him?"

Genie cringed. The last person she wanted to be reminded of was Will. Alex, too, if the tightening of his jaw was any indication.

"I'd met him before."

"He's my favorite quarterback," the second woman gushed.

The elevator door opened with a soft whoosh.

"See you later, Alex." The women got out.

Genie was grateful when the door closed again. "I've always heard big-city neighbors weren't friendly."

"I'd heard the same thing. Guess I got lucky."

Genie remembered the harrumphing sound her fourth-grade teacher used to make when she was displeased. This was definitely a harrumph moment.

The door opened again and Alex guided her down the hallway and into his apartment.

Genie gasped. She walked transfixed into the darkened living room and across it to the windows whose draperies were still pulled back.

Lights glittered from countless windows in all directions. More than the number of people they'd seen today, the lights drove home the staggering differences in the population of Wiley, Georgia, and New York City.

Alex slipped his arms around her from behind, pulling her against him. She sighed and snuggled into the comfort of his arms. This could be dangerously habit-forming.

"Would you like to watch a movie, listen to music or are you ready to call it a night?"

"I'd be happy just looking at this view."

"It's even better upstairs."

She turned in his arms, laughing. "That's not a very subtle attempt at seduction, Alex."

He pulled her hips tightly against him. "I figured if my body was beyond acting subtle, I could be, too."

"Did you now?" She slipped her arms around his neck. "I thought we were going to stretch out on your couch...without our shoes."

He kissed the tender skin below her ear. "There's more room upstairs in my bed."

"How much room do we need?"

"There's also a necessary item of protection upstairs in my nightstand."

"I see."

"Unless you want me to run up there, get it and come back down?"

She didn't want him out of her reach. "That's not necessary."

"Besides, if you come upstairs with me and ask nicely, I may even let you take off more than your shoes."

"That's a real generous offer, Mr. Dalton."

"Shall we go upstairs, then?"

She was about to accept when an unsettling wave of uncertainty crashed over her. She caught her bottom lip between her teeth. "It sounds wonderful..."

He let go of her and stepped back. "Why do I sense a 'but' coming?" Turning, he ran his hands through his hair.

Genie reached out and set her hand on his back. "I'm scared, Alex. There hasn't been anyone since Will."

He turned and took her face between his open palms. "I'll be gentle, angel."

"I know, but..."

She was tempted to keep her worries to herself and let him take her upstairs and make love to her. Maybe it would be different this time. Maybe the trouble hadn't been with her, maybe it had been Will. But was it fair to Alex not to warn him?

She sighed. "You asked one time why Will left me."

"Yes?"

"The bottom line was that I'm not very good at...at making love."

The fire in his eyes flashed an angry blue. "That bastard said that to you?"

She blinked back tears. Maggie didn't even know exactly what Will had said to her to justify his need for other women. "Actually what he said was that I was a poor excuse for a woman and a lousy lay."

He moved away from her again, his fists clenched tightly. He looked like he wanted to drive one of them through something.

Genie took her own step backward. "I'm sorry. I'll just get my suitcase. I don't blame you for being angry. I didn't mean to mislead—"

He blinked, the anger fading from his eyes, then he gathered her to him. Gently, he rocked her, as he had that day in her room. "Shh. I'm not angry at you. I'm angry at Will."

He was angry at Will? She slid her hands underneath his jacket, wrapping her arms around his waist. No doubt about it, cuddling up to this man was definitely habit-forming.

"Genie, did you offer to leave because you don't want to make love or because you think I'll be disappointed?"

How could he imagine she didn't want to? "Because I think you'll be disappointed."

"Then you're not going anywhere." He placed soft kisses on her forehead. "I want you to forget everything Will ever said to you. The man's a fool."

"Alex, why is it that we always end up talking about Will?"

"Because he's a mutual acquaintance?"

"I'm tired of his controlling my life. I'll take responsibility for letting him get away with it up till now, but no more. I don't want to hear his name for the rest of the weekend."

"I'd rather we get him all talked out, so we don't end up with his ghost in bed with us."

"What more is there to talk about?"

"Why don't we sit down?" He led her over to the couch.

She watched him as she slipped out of her shoes. He was trying not to smile, but the dimple gave him away.

"Genie, I think this is important for us to talk about."

"All right." She sat down in the middle of the white leather couch, curling her legs up beneath her.

Alex sat down at one end, leaving a wide space between them. "Since you moved back to Wiley, have any of the men in town asked you out?"

"No. But what does that have to do with Will?"

"Did you ever wonder why they stayed away?"

"I assumed it meant they weren't interested in dating me."

"Genie, Will told them to stay away from you. In fact he told them he's coming back to marry you someday."

She laughed. "Yeah, right. Next you're going to try to sell me the Brooklyn Bridge."

"Kenny told me. Remember the night we were at the gas station?"

She wished she could forget it. "Of course."

"The reason I stopped was that the night before Kenny had threatened me. He'd heard that I'd taken you to dinner and warned me not to see you again."

The whole thing was preposterous. "Will plans to come back and marry me?"

"I doubt he meant the things he said to you."

"If he meant them, I'm sure he wouldn't want to marry me."

"But what if he knew exactly how you would react and said it to manipulate you into going home to Wiley and waiting for him?"

"Then he might come back and ask me to marry him..."

"It would make great press if, after his time in the limelight is over, he goes home and marries the girl next door."

Suddenly it didn't matter what Will had said or why. What she wanted to know was if Alex thought of her that way. "Is that how you see me? As the girl next door?"

Hot sparks of desire were in his eyes again. "No, I see a woman who until recently has hidden the fact that she's beautiful and sexy. Perhaps even hiding it from herself."

"I feel beautiful and sexy when I'm with you...only when I'm with you or getting ready to be with you. I feel alive for the first time in a long time. Thank you."

He smiled. "Glad to be of assistance, angel."

Part of her wanted to seek the safe comfort of the guest room, but the stronger impulse was to pick up where they'd left off.

If he still wanted her....

He broke into her thoughts. "You might end up as Mrs. Will Tucker, after all."

"What makes you think I would accept even if he did offer?"

"It wasn't long ago that I found you crying over a wedding dress."

She nodded. "Yes, but I think that was the beginning of the end. Everything that happened that day helped me to finally accept it was really over."

"Then you wouldn't accept his proposal?"

"No. There's too much hurt and pain associated with our relationship."

"Isn't true love supposed to transcend all that?"

"Theoretically. But looking back, I can't say if I really loved Will or if I loved being in love with Will. He was the captain of the football team, I was head cheerleader. It seemed natural for us to be high school sweethearts and then natural to take the next step beyond that."

"You'll always have that history between you."

"Yes, we will. But I think I'm finally ready to put it to rest. It's time to remember the good times we had but get on with my life."

"Are you sure?"

"Yes."

He reached toward his shoe. "How sure?"

"Very sure."

His shoe hit the floor and was soon joined by its mate.

Nine

Leaving their shoes by the couch, Alex took Genie's hand and led her upstairs. He flicked on the bedroom lights and closed the drapes. "We don't want to enhance anyone else's view," he said. After walking over to the bed, he folded back the spread and blankets.

Genie looked at the wide expanse of sheets. They were smooth now, but she could imagine how they would look tomorrow morning, love-rumpled and warm from the heat of their bodies.

Alex stood on the opposite side. He held out his hand to her. Slowly, she walked around the foot of the bed.

When she reached him, he unbuttoned her jacket, slipped it off and tossed it on the end of the mattress.

Looking down, she noticed the wetness on her blouse had dried. But the memory of how it had gotten there made her breasts ache and her nipples pull tight enough to be visible through the fabric covering them.

One by one, Alex released each of her buttons. "I used to fantasize about this, Genie." His voice was rougher than usual, his breathing labored. "About how I'd undress you slowly, then sink myself deep into you. It was heavy torment for a testosterone-laden teenager."

"I never suspected."

"I had it bad, angel." He let her blouse slide down her arms and flutter to the floor behind her. He shrugged out of his jacket and laid it by hers, then reached for his tie. "I would lie awake at night thinking about you. Once I fell asleep, I dreamed about you. And when I woke up in the morning—"

"You . . . you never said anything."

"Would I have had a chance with you back then?"

"I . . ." She wished she could tell him yes, but they would both know she was lying. "Probably not, but it was definitely my loss."

His hands, which had been unbuttoning his shirt, stilled. She took over the task, pulling out the shirttails so she could get all the buttons. He held each arm up and she unbuttoned his cuffs. Working together, they added his shirt and her bra to the growing collection on the floor.

As she reached for his belt and he reached for the hook on her slacks, he moved closer to her and brought his mouth down over hers. Somehow they managed to discard the rest of their clothing.

Genie felt the world tilt. When cool sheets touched her back, she realized Alex had moved them onto the bed. Her eyes fluttered open. Alex was next to her. But as she watched, he turned, moving his weight over her until they lay touching along the length of their bodies.

She'd thought nothing could feel better than being held in his arms, but she'd been wrong. The absence of intrusive cloth between them and the extra pressure gravity provided sent her senses reeling.

Alex lowered his head to kiss the tender skin of her neck. She arched, giving him better access. Reaching around his broad shoulders, she ran her hands over the hard surface of his back.

He looked at her, intense desire burning in his eyes. Holding her gaze, he slid his body downward until he was level with her breasts. Gently, he teased one with his hand and one with his mouth.

"Watch the nails, angel."

Genie realized her fingers had curled inward to clutch at his back. "Sorry."

He slid even lower, placing feather-soft kisses in places, lingering longer in others. When he reached the gentle swell of her womanhood, between the skill of his mouth and fingers, Genie felt as if she was about to shatter.

"Alex, hurry, please. I can't wait."

"Don't wait."

"But—"

He shifted his hand and Genie tumbled over the edge. She let herself fall. As if from a distance, she could hear Alex murmuring approval and coaxing her on and on. As she floated in sweet afterglow, Alex began his gentle ministering again. By the time he'd worked his way up her body, her hunger for him had rebuilt to a fever pitch.

After reaching over to open the nightstand drawer, he finally adjusted their lower bodies so he was poised, ready to enter her.

"Open your eyes, Genie."

She did as he asked, watching the play of emotions across his face as he joined them together. He wore the look of the conqueror about to receive his reward, yet at the same time the countenance of a benefactor offering a gift.

They continued to watch each other as Alex set a slow steady rhythm, which Genie followed. As one, they climbed the plateau and, when it was time, went over the edge together.

Alex reached up and flipped off the bedside lights, then settled down to hold Genie in the dark. Her hair was fanned across his chest and her warm breath blew softly across his damp skin.

"Comfortable, angel?"

"Umm." Her breathing had slowed. Alex suspected she was about to drift off to sleep.

Sleep was the last thing on his mind.

Making love to her had rocked him to his soul. And as if the intense sexual satisfaction wasn't enough, he now felt an incredible, unfamiliar peace.

He felt that nothing was more important at this moment than for him to be holding Genie. All of the demands that Yankee made on him would wait. This was where he needed to be and what he needed to be doing.

As he lay there, he stored memories of the feel of her, the faint lingering scent of her shampoo, the soft sounds of contentment she made as she nestled closer to him.

Surely all her doubts about her abilities as a lover were laid to rest now. He didn't understand how she could have believed Will when he'd told her that. Unless Will was a lousy lover, as well as a jerk.

She'd be more sure of herself next time she got involved with someone. Maybe she would remember tonight as a turning point for the rest of her life. He would be firmly embedded in her memory as more than the nerd who had helped her pass algebra.

A wave of discontentment passed through him. He didn't like the idea of some other man touching her, bringing her pleasure.

Careful, Alex, you're starting to sound possessive. Not a wise move.

Not part of his plan...

The plan called for more of tonight's pleasures and then to send her on her way. He would focus on the first step and worry about the rest of it when the time came.

Genie woke slowly. Expecting to be in warm arms, as she had been when she'd awakened during the night, she was surprised to find herself alone. She yawned and stretched.

How could Alex be up already? They'd made love several more times during the night, and she felt as if she could sleep a few more hours, at least.

But she also wanted to see Alex. She could catch up on her sleep on the flight home.

Flight home.

The words chilled her. *Don't think about it now.* There would be plenty of time to deal with it later. She didn't want to waste any of the time she had with Alex.

After a quick shower in the spacious master bathroom, she slipped into the silky robe she found hanging on the back of the door. The large sunken whirlpool tub beckoned, but it would be even nicer with Alex, so it would wait.

She found Alex in the oversize leather chair behind his desk. His hair was tumbled over his forehead and his jaw was darkened by morning stubble. He wore a pair of wire frame glasses, and from her position by the doorway, it looked as though that might be all he was wearing.

Her heart raced. When he looked up and smiled at her, it tripped into overdrive.

"Morning, angel. Sleep well?"

"Yes. Did you?"

"Like a baby."

Genie walked over to stand in front of the desk. From here she could see Alex was wearing a pair of sweatpants low on his hips. She wasn't sure whether she was relieved or disappointed. Spread across the smooth desktop were assorted photos. Featured in them were the same red, white and blue motorcycles and riders in matching leather that were in the famous ad.

"Thinking about revealing their identities, after all?"

"No. Our ad exec has suggested expanding the campaign and using other shots along with the original."

Genie picked up a photo. The biker in blue leather was the only one in the shot with the blue motorcycle, although the red and white bikes were in the background. Even with the man's face hidden, his body language spoke loud and clear—one-hundred-percent genuine sexy male.

"See anything you like, angel?"

The sound of Alex's voice broke into her wayward thoughts. She felt her cheeks grow warm. How could she be close to drooling over some guy in a photo when she had an equally sexy male right in the same room with her? "This one's nice." She handed the photo to Alex.

He looked at it, a tiny smile inexplicably playing across his face. Then he gathered up the photos and put them in a file folder. "So, ready for breakfast?"

Working together in the state-of-the-art kitchen, they had things ready in no time. Seated side by side at the table in the breakfast nook, they gave more of their attention to each other than to the food.

After a long, lingering kiss, Alex said, "I think we should save room for Thanksgiving dinner."

"Good idea."

Alex smiled. It was one of his sexy smiles, the kind that emphasized his dimple.

Genie stroked one finger across the dimple on his cheek. "You know, I never got a good look at that other dimple you mentioned."

"You didn't?"

"No."

"I can fix that."

They only made it as far as the guest room, and Genie was surprised they made it that far.

Their lovemaking last night had been incredible. Unbelievably, it kept getting better and better. They even tried out the tub in the master bathroom before dressing for the afternoon Thanksgiving party.

Alex's friend lived in the building next door, so they covered more distance vertically than horizontally.

"Whatever happened to over the river and through the woods?" Genie asked as they headed up in the elevator.

"This isn't Wiley." His expression turned serious. "How does your family feel about you being away for the holiday?"

She shrugged. "They weren't too happy. But I really needed some time away. I haven't been any farther than Atlanta since I moved back, and I needed a change of scenery." *And I needed to see you again.* "What about your family? Do you usually spend Thanksgiving with them?"

"It depends. Sometimes I go to California to be with my parents, other times we go to Wiley, but since we were all there last month for Grandee's birthday, I decided to stay here this year."

The elevator opened and Alex escorted her down the hallway. His knock was answered almost immediately and they entered another beautifully decorated apartment. It looked as though it might be about the same size as Alex's, but it was hard to tell with the large number of people milling around.

Anytime Genie and Will had attended a large social gathering, he'd usually wandered off after fifteen minutes or so, leaving her on her own.

Alex stayed by her side, one hand possessively on her back or around her shoulder. He introduced her to people he knew, sent her smoldering glances and seemed happy to be with her.

More guests kept arriving. One of them was Alex's partner, Jesse. He came over to them shortly after he arrived.

"How do you like New York so far, Genie?"

"I'm having a wonderful time."

"Good. Alex being a good host?"

Genie felt a warm rush of blood to her cheeks. "Yes."

Jesse smiled. A knowing spark lit his green eyes. "Glad to hear it."

Another couple came up and while Alex was introducing them to her, Genie noticed Jesse slip away. After that, every time she spotted him, there was a different woman lurking nearby, hanging on to his every word. She wondered if the same would be true for Alex if she wasn't there with him.

After a trip through the buffet line, they found a table for two tucked away in a corner.

"I had meant to ask you last night if you wanted to go to the Thanksgiving parade this morning," Alex said.

"I'm sure the parade was wonderful, but I have no complaints about the way we spent the morning." They exchanged an intimate look.

"Good."

After eating, they socialized a little more, then headed back to Alex's.

Over the next two days, they discussed a variety of sight-seeing outings and things to do, but ended up not leaving the apartment until Saturday night and only then because Alex insisted that a trip to New York wasn't complete without a Broadway show.

They spent Sunday in long, languid hours of lovemaking until it was time for her to pack. Alex, in casual pants and sweater, lay on top of the recently made bed, watching her.

Genie didn't want to go home. She couldn't remember when she'd felt so alive...so full of joy...so cherished. Alex made her feel cherished. Cherished and special.

Why couldn't she have fallen in love with a man like this?

Oh, but you have.... You've fallen hard.

The thought recurred over and over as she finished packing, as they drove to the airport. When had it happened? When had she fallen in love with Alex?

And what a time to realize it...when it was time to leave. But it felt like she'd just arrived. At the same time it felt like she'd been there a lifetime.

At the boarding gate, Alex kissed her.

When he straightened and looked down at her, she said, "I love you, Alex." She hadn't meant to blurt it out this way, but once it was out, she couldn't take it back.

Alex ran his fingertips along the side of her face. "I promised you a weekend to remember—"

She didn't want to hear his platitudes to let her down easy. Forcing a smile, she interrupted him. "You gave me that. Thank you. I'm not asking for more. I just wanted to tell you how I feel."

He frowned. "Even if I don't return the sentiment?"

"Yes. But don't worry about me, I'm real good at loving men who don't love me back." She put her arms around his neck and pulled him to her for one last kiss. "Thanks again for the weekend."

Before he could respond, she stepped back, picked up her garment bag and headed for the door.

Genie walked down the jetway, her head held high. She'd gone into the weekend with her eyes wide open, she reminded herself. So she wasn't going to cry or mope.

She did allow herself to wonder if she was capable of making a healthy choice of a male partner. Will had been a major mistake. And it looked like getting involved with Alex might have been a mistake, too.

At least Alex had seemed satisfied with their lovemaking. And surely the quantity as well as the quality of their times together should count for something.

Yet it seemed so easy for him to send her home.

She only allowed herself a moment of disappointment that the incredible lovemaking between them hadn't changed Alex's mind about wanting a relationship. Other than that, she allowed herself no regrets.

And if she repeated it often enough, she might begin to believe it.

Alex stared at the street below, watching the cars creep by.

He'd done it. Victory was his. Genie Hill was in love with him.

But where was the euphoria?

An unsettling thought came to him. He'd expected to feel so happy when he told her he didn't return her feelings, but the more he went over it, he realized the biggest thrill had come when she'd looked at him and said those four words—I love you, Alex.

He imagined what it would be like to hear them first thing in the morning and last thing at night. He envisioned her repeating the words over and over again in the throes of passion, her voice husky and breathless.

He swore darkly as he felt a physical response to his wayward thoughts. A cold shower would help, but only if he could keep from thinking about how he'd made love to Genie there and in the nearby tub.

On the other hand, he did want to think about it. Think about it and remember every last erotic detail.

Genie fell back into her regular work routine, but every night she fought the urge to pick up the phone and call Alex.

She couldn't help wondering if she would ever see him again. Would he call next time he came to see Grandee? Would he be coming soon?

Everyone at school loved her new haircut and more stylish clothes. She and Maggie went shopping one afternoon after class and Genie expanded her new wardrobe even more.

The first Saturday after her trip, she spent cleaning house until everything shone. She showered, changed into a pair of sweats and curled up on the couch with a book and a mug of herbal tea.

When the phone rang, she suspected it might be Maggie wanting her to baby-sit her nephews for the evening. But it was Alex's voice on the line.

"How are you, angel?"

"I'm fine." Well, she was trying hard to be fine and hearing his voice made her feel better. "How are you?"

"I miss you."

She clutched the phone with both hands to keep from dropping it. "You miss me?"

"Yes, I do."

"I don't know what to say."

"You could tell me you miss me, too," he suggested.

"I've missed you, Alex."

"What are we going to do about it?"

"I don't see what we can do."

"How about if I come down there next weekend?"

Slipping off to New York for a clandestine weekend was one thing, but having him stay with her here in full view of all her friends and relatives was something else. Unless he'd changed his mind and wanted more than just a physical relationship. "I don't know. The neighbors—"

"Listen. I'll stay at Grandee's overnight if you think there will be problems if I stay with you. But I really want to see you, angel."

"Why?"

"We'll talk about it when I get there."

He wouldn't go through all the trouble of coming to Wiley to tell her he didn't want to see her again, would he?

Early Tuesday morning, Alex strode into his office and slammed the door. Jesse was wearing a suit, lounging on the couch in the conversation pit. Rorke, in blue jeans, T-shirt and black leather jacket, was standing by the window behind the desk.

"In a bad mood, Dalton?" Jesse asked.

Rorke turned to face Alex. "Seen a morning paper?"

"I hadn't until I had one shoved in my face in the lobby." The tabloid headline had read, Fantasy Bikers Revealed. He set his briefcase next to his desk. "Any idea how word got out?"

Jesse sat up straighter. "We thought you might have the answer to that."

At one time, Alex had been trying to convince Rorke and Jesse to go public with their identities. "I had nothing to do with this. If you'd agreed to my suggestion to go public, it would have been a well-orchestrated campaign—I'd suggested bike week, remember?"

He picked up the phone. "Rose, get me Russell on the phone." He looked over at Rorke. "My guess is that Mike Maxwell got to someone at the agency."

He'd returned Maxwell's call the day after he'd returned from Wiley. Maxwell had asked for an exclusive on the billboard models' identities—again. Alex refused and Maxwell repeated his implication that he would find out on his own.

Alex had considered notifying the ad agency then, but hadn't. He wondered if it would have prevented the current dilemma. It was almost a certainty that Maxwell's source was someone at the agency. At this point, though, more important than finding out how their identities were leaked, was deciding how he could handle it to the company's best advantage.

Tuesday evening, Genie was at her sister's house for dinner. She was in the kitchen refilling her coffee mug when Maggie called out, "Genie, get in here. Fast!"

Genie ran into the family room. Maggie was pointing to the television. On the screen were three motorcycles positioned between cameras and lighting equipment.

"The man said this was footage taken the day of the shoot for the Yankee ads. Apparently they were working on a TV commercial and the billboard."

As they watched, three helmeted, leather-clad men moved into the scene. The photographer positioned them and began shooting. In the distance a phone rang.

"All right, let's take a fifteen-minute break," a male voice shouted off camera.

One by one the bikers removed their helmets. The film was frozen, moved in for a close-up shot and a name flashed on the screen beneath each handsome face. Jesse Tyler. Rorke O'Neil. Alex Dalton.

"There they are, ladies. The Yankee hunks. The bad news is that Rorke O'Neil is a recent newlywed...the good news is that Jesse and Alex are single. The story broke this morning when the tape you just saw was sold to a local newspaper reporter. So far there has been no official statement from Yankee. In a clip from earlier

today, the three men are seen here leaving their headquarters.''

The film clip showed a swarm of women and photographers being held back by a barricade. Alex, Jesse
and Rorke were whisked into a limousine. As the door
was being closed, Alex looked right at the camera and
waved.

Maggie shook her head. "That man is too studly for
his own good."

Genie managed a weak smile. She remembered the
morning she'd found Alex with the pictures scattered
over his desk. It would have been the perfect time for
him to tell her. But he hadn't.

She realized that somewhere inside, she'd been hoping part of him had been falling in love with her, too—
but if he hadn't trusted her with his secret, then that
scenario seemed doubtful.

And from the film clip, she'd seen he was the one in
blue, the one in the picture she'd been admiring. No
wonder he'd seemed amused.

The tabloid show moved on to the next tidbit of
gossip. Maggie turned off the TV. "Has Alex called
you or anything since you came home?"

Genie had told her sister she'd seen Alex on her trip,
but not any of the details. Not even that she had stayed
in his apartment.

"Actually I spoke to him on Saturday."

"Did he say anything about this?" She waved one
hand in the direction of the television.

"Not a word." Surely if he cared about her, he would have told her.

As he'd pointed out to her at the airport, all he'd promised was a weekend to remember. The problem was, she hadn't truly believed him.

She believed him now.

Genie had been home about half an hour when the phone rang.

It was Alex.

They exchanged greetings, then Alex said, "Angel, I'm not going to be able to make it this weekend."

Ten

"I didn't think you would."

Now that Alex was in high demand, why would he bother with her? From what she'd seen on TV, women were standing in line to throw themselves at his feet. He could have his pick...just like Will when he'd been drafted into the NFL.

She thought about what she'd learned from Jesse. How Alex still had his pocket protector in graduate school. That would give him even more years of unpopularity to make up for. With his new star status, he would probably be like a chocoholic in a candy store.

"Word's out all the way down there?" he asked.

"It was on the evening tabloid shows. Word's out nationwide."

"Damn."

"They showed you, Rorke and Jesse leaving the office today."

"That was a nightmare."

He'd looked happy enough, smiling and waving to the camera. She wanted to ask why he hadn't told her. Instead she said, "Well, I won't keep you. I'm sure you must be busy."

"I lost work time today, which I'm hoping to make up this evening. I'll try to make it down there next weekend."

Would it really be work that filled the extra hours for him? She felt as though she'd woken up to find herself in the nightmare that was her last few months with Will. Did she want to relive all the uncertainties and suspicions?

The time alone wondering what woman was making him an offer. The torture of not knowing when one would come up with an offer he couldn't refuse. Then the accusations that if she was a better lover, he wouldn't have been tempted.

It had all happened with Will. Did she want to take the chance of it happening again with Alex?

"There's really no need to bother. Unless you're coming to visit your family."

"I'm coming to see you."

Genie took a deep breath and let it out slowly. "I don't think it's a good idea for us to see each other anymore."

There was a pause, then Alex said, "Isn't that a strange remark from someone who said she's in love with me?"

"Since you don't return the feeling, what difference does it make?" She hung up the phone.

Alex recruited several members of the typing pool to help his secretary deal with the increase in phone calls and mail.

Thursday morning, they set four piles of letters across the front of his desk.

His secretary, Rose, pointed to each in turn. "Business correspondence, requests for interviews and personal appearances, general fan mail and marriage proposals."

"Marriage proposals?"

Rose shrugged. "It's hard work being a sex symbol."

Laughing, Alex picked up the top letter in the last pile and began to read it. "This *is* a marriage proposal." He picked up the rest of the pile and flipped through it. "You weren't joking."

"I wouldn't joke about something like this."

Alex shook his head in amazement. Life was strange and unpredictable. Alexander Lee Dalton, once a misfit, now every woman's fantasy man...

Go figure.

Of course he wasn't *every* woman's fantasy man. He was no longer Genie's. Although she hadn't actually said she didn't love him anymore, she'd made it clear she wasn't interested in seeing him again.

Don't let it bother you. You were only going to see her a few more times anyway.

Yes, but he was supposed to be the one to call it quits. He would think of something. But at the moment he had work to do.

Alex had the business correspondence and phone calls handled by noon, so when Jesse walked in and asked if he'd like to go to lunch, he accepted.

They went to a local restaurant they frequented often enough that they didn't have to wait in line to be seated.

It wasn't unusual for them to attract female attention—covert glances and women whispering to each other—but today the stares were obvious, accompanied by come-hither smiles and a few blatant winks.

Jesse shook his head. "I know it's only been a little over forty-eight hours, but this is getting old."

Alex didn't share Jesse's opinion. He soaked up the attention. Using it to once more soothe over the visions of the lonely teenager his trip to Wiley had stirred up. "It seems as though every woman I've dated or exchanged phone numbers with is trying to renew our acquaintance. Not to mention the new ones that seem to be materializing out of thin air."

"Same here."

The waiter arrived and took their order. Once they were alone again, Jesse asked, "Have you gone out with any of them yet?"

"Who's got time?" Alex took a sip of water. "From the smile on your face, obviously you have."

"It's not *that* kind of smile, Dalton."

"Did you take one out or not?"

"I did, last night. After dinner we went back to my place. I was picking out a few CDs and I thought she'd slipped off to the bathroom to freshen up. But I found her going through my closet looking for the red leather pants and jacket I'd worn in the ad. She wanted me to make love to her wearing them."

Alex laughed. "With or without the boots and helmet?"

"She didn't say, but she was real disappointed when I told her the outfit wasn't mine."

"Maybe you should get yourself a set."

Jesse scowled at him. "How much fun do you think it would be making love to a woman who wanted my image as a Yankee hunk rather than me?"

Alex hadn't looked at it that way. He'd let his ego be fed by the flood of attention—let the lonely teenager he'd been wallow in it. But the women who'd been chasing him were only chasing that billboard image, too. "It doesn't sound much fun when you put it that way."

A pretty blonde in a tight dress came up to their table. "Excuse me, but aren't you two of those Yankee guys?"

Alex and Jesse exchanged glances.

The blonde continued, "Could I have your autographs?" She pulled a paper and pen from her purse.

Jesse signed first. Alex could tell from the tightness of Jesse's smile that he was not happy. To compensate, Alex flirted with the woman when it was his turn to sign.

As soon as the woman had gone, Jesse turned to Alex. "I've had enough of this. I'll fly down to Florida tonight. I'm going to bury myself in the lab and play with some new alloys until this chaos settles down."

Lunch arrived, but Alex had lost his appetite.

By Friday afternoon, Alex was tired—more than tired, exhausted. And he was craving more than the peace of sleep. He wanted the deep peace he'd felt after making love to Genie.

Maybe he would take the time to go to Georgia for the weekend, after all.

Friday night, Genie was putting her dinner dishes in the dishwasher when the doorbell rang.

"Alex!"

"Hi. I was in the neighborhood and thought I'd stop by."

Against her better judgment, she opened the door and stepped back to let him in. Once he was inside, she noticed how tired he looked.

He flashed her a crooked, boyish smile. "I've had a hell of a week."

"You look exhausted."

He reached out and took her into his arms. "And you look beautiful."

Genie sighed and settled her cheek against the hard wall of his chest. Her knees felt wobbly and a familiar throbbing need started within her. "Alex, this is not a good idea."

"I'm just holding you."

"All you're going to do is hold me?"

"It's completely up to you."

She tilted her head and looked at him. "Up to me?"

He lowered his head until his mouth hovered just above hers. "Absolutely."

The word whispered across her lips. The memories of their passionate lovemaking flooded her thoughts. She reached her arms around his neck and closed the distance between them. The feel and taste of him pervaded her senses and she knew she was lost.

All her good intentions of staying clear of him and protecting herself from a broken heart blew away like chalk dust.

She parted her lips and traced the firm line of his with her tongue. He opened for her and she deepened the kiss. He groaned and pulled her hips tightly against him. The invitation to go beyond kisses was clear.

Genie knew she would regret it in the morning... or whenever he headed back to the Big Apple and his adoring public. She would regret it, but she was going to do it anyway.

After all, he was here and he wanted her and whether it was in her best interests or not, she wanted him.

She pulled back. "Would you like to go upstairs?"

"If you do."

Genie turned off the living room lights, took him by the hand and led him upstairs.

They left articles of clothing along the way, shedding the last barriers before they tumbled, laughing from the sheer joy of being together, into the soft comfort of her bed.

The lonely hours of their time apart disappeared as once again they exchanged passionate kisses and urgent caresses.

Genie tried to take it slowly, savor each moment, but her body seemed to have its own idea. "Now. Please, Alex, now."

"Now what, angel?"

"Make love to me now."

He flicked his tongue over the tight peak of her breast. "I've been making love to you."

"Don't tease. You know what I mean."

He positioned himself to enter her, but held back. "Tell me what you want."

She moved against him. "I want you."

He entered her at last.

She cried out his name.

They fell into a mutual rhythm of give and take, advance and retreat. There was a frenzied edge to tonight's lovemaking, which hadn't been there in New York.

"I love you," Genie murmured seconds before she was caught in the grip of an intense climax.

Alex joined her, driving them both until they were drained, then turning them so she rested over him.

The mind-numbing ecstasy subsided. A sinking feeling settled in the pit of Genie's stomach. The regrets hadn't waited for morning.

What have you done, Genie?

She'd declared her love again, and again Alex hadn't returned the sentiment.

She looked at him.

He smiled. A slow, sexy, triumphant smile.

"I... I think you'd better go."

Both brows rose in surprise. "Excuse me?"

She untangled herself from him and sat up on the edge of the bed, gathering the quilt around her.

Didn't she have any pride? Not only had she tumbled into bed with him, but she'd declared her love again, knowing he didn't share her feelings. "I didn't mean for this to happen."

"I didn't mean for this to happen, either. Not tonight. Angel, I was exhausted when I got here. Now, after *this*, I can't even keep my eyes open. Turn off the lights and come to bed."

He just wanted to sleep.

They needed to talk.

She needed to make him understand that loving him the way she did, it hurt her to be with him knowing he didn't love her back.

He yawned and nestled into her pillow. "Have a heart, angel."

She had one ... it was breaking.

The next morning, Genie woke to the aroma of freshly brewed coffee. Alex was propped up next to her, sipping from a mug and reading the Wiley *Gazette.* Today's edition.

"Where did you get that?"

"The paperboy tossed it on your driveway. Well, it landed in the hedge, but luckily Mrs. Craig saw it land so she knew right where it was."

Oh, Lord, no! "Mrs. Craig?"

"Yeah, you know, your next-door neighbor." He set the mug on the nightstand, folded the paper and placed it on the floor. "Are you feeling all right? You look a little pale."

"You were outside this morning, talking to my neighbor?"

"Neighbors, actually. Mrs. Johnson was out planting her bulbs for next spring."

Genie wanted to crawl far beneath the covers and never come out. "I can't believe you did this to me!" She buried her face in her pillow.

"You've stopped looking like a schoolmarm. Don't you want everyone to know you've stopped acting like one?"

"Definitely not. It's none of their business . . . or my parents'. . . or my sister's. You know this will be all over town. In fact it will probably make the next edition of the *Gazette.*"

Alex laughed.

"This isn't funny."

"Oh, yes, it is." He kept laughing.

"I can't believe what deplorable taste I have in men. First Will, now you."

Alex stopped laughing. Anger replaced the mirth on his face. "That's hitting below the belt. I don't appreciate it."

"And I don't appreciate your letting my neighbors see you coming out of my house early in the morning." A thought struck her. She looked up. Alex had the sheet pulled up to his trim waist. Everything above it was bare. "What were you wearing when you went outside, Alex?"

The anger faded slowly and he flashed her a wicked smile. "Nothing."

"Nothing?"

"Nothing," he repeated, this time imitating her accent.

She moaned. "I. . .now. . ." She started to stand, but Alex reached up and pulled her into his arms.

"Now? Well, all right, but wouldn't you like me to get you a little warmed up first?"

"I want you out of here now!" She struggled to get out of his arms, but he easily reversed their positions until she was beneath him.

"Shh." With his hands, he gently stroked her hair from her face. "Settle down, Genie. I'm only teasing."

"Teasing?"

"Yes. I said I wore nothing outside because I didn't go outside."

"But the paper?"

"It's raining. The paperboy put it through the mail slot in your door."

Genie listened. Yes, there it was. The gentle patter of raindrops on the roof. She caught her bottom lip between her teeth and slowly shook her head from side to side. "I feel like a complete idiot."

Alex looked thoughtful as he moved his hands down to run over her body. "I think you feel terrific. Soft, warm and seductive." He placed a feather-light kiss on her lips. "I'm sorry I teased you. But you got the strangest look on your face when you saw the paper. I guessed what you were thinking. And since you're so adorable when you're flustered, I couldn't resist."

"I'm sorry I jumped to so many conclusions."

"You should have known I wouldn't deliberately set out to embarrass you in front of your neighbors. I even left my rental car at Grandee's and walked over, so they wouldn't know I was here."

She remembered how angry he'd looked when she'd likened him to Will. "I'm sorry I compared you to Will."

"I'm nothing like Will, Genie."

Except they were both currently in the public eye and were lusted after by throngs of adoring women. They needed to talk about it. But lying naked beneath him was not the best place to carry on a serious conversation.

And once he lowered his head and pressed his mouth over hers, there wasn't any conversation at all.

It was past breakfast time when they finally got downstairs.

"So what shall we do today?" Alex asked as he helped Genie throw together a light brunch.

"I think we need to talk."

"Uh-oh, sounds serious. Don't we have enough serious time during the week, playing teacher and businessman?"

"But you're not just a businessman anymore. You're a national phenomenon." Genie set the pitcher of orange juice on the table, then stood next to Alex as he spread butter on toast. "Why didn't you tell me you were in the ad?"

He shrugged. "It didn't seem important."

"Not important?"

"We weren't planning to go public with it, so I didn't think it was any big deal."

"No big deal? When you need barricades to hold the women back when you leave your office?"

"I never expected that kind of reaction."

"You had the perfect opportunity to tell me that morning in New York when you were looking at the pictures."

"It didn't seem necessary."

"Even at that point in our relationship?"

"Ah-ha!" He set down the knife and turned to face her. "That's where the problem is. In the two different ways we define our relationship."

Genie thought about it a few moments. "I guess you're right. Expecting you to share that kind of information with me assumes there is an established relationship between us and you're just into showing me a good time."

He turned back to the counter. "It's not like I didn't warn you."

"I know."

"You were okay with it when you got on the plane."

"I know."

"And you seemed okay with it when I called to say I was coming down for the weekend. Why did the announcement that I'm in the ad change things?"

Genie walked over and sat down at the kitchen table, propping her chin on her fist. She felt sure the answer to his question was all that had happened with Will. But she knew better than to mention his name again. "I'm not sure. But it did."

Alex came up behind her. Placing his hands on her shoulders, he began a gentle massage across the top of her back and up her neck.

She closed her eyes and let the motions soothe her. "The first time you called and said you were coming to Wiley, you said we had to talk." She'd let herself imagine he wanted to tell her he'd discovered he did love her after all.

"I wanted to talk about making arrangements for us to spend some time together, coordinate Christmas vacations, make plans for New Year's Eve."

"You want us to spend more time together?"

"Of course."

Could he be falling in love with her? "Why?"

"Why does any man want to spend time with a woman?"

"Either because he enjoys her company or because he wants to take her to bed."

"Well, in this case, I'd have to go with all of the above."

"Do you still want to? Even now that you're a national attraction?"

"Mount Rushmore is a national attraction. Ever been there?"

"You're changing the subject."

"Because I don't think I can give you the answer you're looking for."

Had he guessed what she wanted to hear was that she was the only woman in the world for him, that none of the other women mattered, that he loved her and only her?

She remembered back to the night they'd had dinner at the Wiley Café. He'd offered her a fast fling.

Apparently what he was offering was an extended version of the same thing...an affair. She needed to learn to live with the idea or put her foot down and refuse to see him again.

And if last night was any indication of how well she could do that, she didn't stand a chance.

Eleven

Genie managed to get through the rest of the weekend by resolving to live for the moment. If there was any hope at all that Alex might fall in love with her, it wouldn't happen if she was moping or begging. So she set out to enjoy the time they had together and leave all mention of love out of the picture.

It helped that Alex was fun to be with. The hours seemed to fly by.

After making love Saturday night, Genie turned off the lights and they lay snuggled together in the darkness. "I was wondering about something. You said you had a crush on me as a teenager."

"I did."

"Then when my mother invited you to my party, why didn't you come?"

Alex was quiet. Genie had decided he must have fallen asleep when he finally spoke.

"After I started for Grandee's, I decided to go back and talk to your mom, try to get some gift ideas, see if I could outdo Will. When I got there, you and your mother were arguing."

A sick feeling settled in her stomach. "And you heard us."

She felt him take a deep breath.

"Yes." His voice was quiet, nothing in its tone giving away any clue to his emotions.

"I remember the incident, but I don't remember what I said. What did I say, Alex?"

"That was a long time ago."

"It was, but you remember what I said, don't you?"

"Yes."

Genie sat up, pulling her knees to her chest and wrapping her arms around them. "Whatever I said hurt you, didn't it?"

"Yes."

Will's remark about revenge being a powerful motivator came into her mind. She suspected revenge might have been Alex's motive in his pursuit of her the week of Grandee's birthday. Not revenge against Will...

Revenge against her.

"I'm sorry," she said into the darkness. "I wish I could say I didn't mean whatever it was I said, but I'm afraid the best I can do is say that I never would have said it to your face and I never would have said it if I'd known you were listening."

Alex placed his hand on her back. "Lie down, angel, and let's get some sleep."

She lay down. He wrapped his arms around her, holding her close.

"I really am sorry, Alex."

"It was a long time ago. It's over and done with." He was still using the same quiet, unemotional tone of voice.

Genie tried to remember the argument she'd had with her mother that summer afternoon. She remembered being angry that her mother had invited Alex, upset about what her friends would say, but little else.

Except . . . a word danced on the fringe of her memories. Nerd. She'd called him a nerd and she was sure that it would have been very clear to anyone listening that she hadn't wanted him at her party.

How that must have hurt him.

And he'd been on his way to talk to her mother about gift ideas for her, trying to compete with Will.

Will had been good-looking and popular. Surely Alex should have realized how futile his hopes had been. But he'd liked her enough to try.

Until her own words had made him change his mind.

They were both more subdued on Sunday, but whether it was the impending separation or last night's conversation that was to blame, Genie wasn't sure.

Alex told her he needed to leave around noon. Genie walked him to the door. Topmost in her mind was the thought that they had never gotten around to discussing when they would see each other next.

Maybe Alex had changed his mind.

She was still puzzled by the question of revenge. It had seemed logical in the dark of night to suspect it. But in the clear light of day, she wasn't sure Alex was capable of seeking revenge. The deed seemed incongruous with the way he was such a considerate lover and the caring way he had with Grandee.

She didn't know *what* to believe.

At the door, he took her in his arms and kissed her goodbye. "Love me, angel?"

There was that word she'd deliberately avoided saying out loud since Friday night. If Alex was out for revenge, it might take some of the wind out of his sails if she could convince him that she didn't. "I, um, I've been thinking. Maybe I was a little hasty when I said it," she lied. "My days in New York were very surprising—"

His smile faded. "Surprising? An interesting word choice."

"Surprising and enlightening. Overwhelming even." She managed a smile. "Bright lights, big city, the heat of passion. I'm sure you don't need me to tell you what a terrific lover you are." When he didn't answer, she continued, "You gave me back my self-respect. I'll always be grateful for that, Alex."

He laughed. "Grateful?"

"Yes."

"You're grateful." His grip on her tightened. "Damn it, Genie, I don't want your gratitude. I want you to want me, I want you to need me, I want you to love me."

Was his need motivated by revenge? "Why?"

"You said you did in New York. And you said it Friday night."

"I know what I said."

"Say it again."

"Why?"

"I want to hear you say it again."

"So you can throw it back in my face? You can at least let me have some pride, Alex. Isn't it enough that women all over the country are lusting after you?"

He looked at her, an uncharacteristic coldness in the blue depths of his eyes. "Maybe it should be." He turned toward the door.

"Alex?"

He looked over his shoulder.

Don't say something you're going to regret. "Did you start asking me out as retaliation? Because I didn't consider you potential date material when we were teenagers?"

He came back to stand in front of her. "Do you want the truth?"

Genie hesitated. Was she prepared to hear this? She nodded. "Yes."

"I'm not especially proud of it." He took a deep breath and let it out slowly. "But, yes, that's why I asked you out."

Once the words had been spoken a wave of hurt, anger and disappointment washed over her. Mostly it stung her ego and her pride.

Genie wanted to make him take back his words. Make him say he'd asked her out because he'd had such a strong crush on her as a teenager that he hadn't been able to get her out of his mind.

But, she reminded herself, looking the way she had when he'd arrived, she wouldn't have stood a chance of attracting him. Without being driven by the need for revenge, would he have worked at removing the schoolmarm facade, helping her discover the beautiful, sensuous woman hidden beneath? Probably not.

And they would never have found the special magic they made together. Magic whose memories she would carry a lifetime. "Thank you for being honest."

His mouth was a grim line. "I guess I owe you at least that much."

She shrugged. "Well, you know the way out." After turning her back, she left the room.

Tuesday morning, the phone in Alex's office rang yet again. He picked it up. "Hello."

"Alex Dalton?"

"Yes, may I help you?"

"Alex, this is Adrienne Stanfield. We went to high school together."

He had thought of Adrienne last month on his trip to Wiley. She was the first girl he'd asked out. Genie would have been the first if he hadn't let Will dissuade him. So Adrienne had been the first. She had given him a you-must-be-kidding look and walked away.

"Yes, Adrienne, what can I do for you?"

"I saw you on TV the other night. At first I didn't realize it was you, but then the local station did a special profile."

He wished he could have seen her reaction. "Still in southern California?"

"Yes, and if you get out this way to visit your parents, I want you to give me a call."

"Sure." *Don't hold your breath, Adrienne.*

"I know this great little restaurant—"

This was interesting. "You're asking me out to dinner?"

"Yes, if you still want to."

"Still want to? Adrienne, I asked you out the summer after we graduated from high school. And you looked at me like I was something that had gotten stuck to the bottom of your shoe."

"Oh, you know how it is in high school. Peer pressure and all that. I really did like you and all, but I was afraid of what everyone would say if they saw us out together. You know how cruel teenagers can be."

Did he ever! He wasn't buying her I-was-a-victim-of-circumstances excuse. At least Genie had been honest about the past. She'd admitted that she wouldn't have gone out with him if he'd asked and that she'd meant the words she'd said to her mother, even though she didn't remember what they were. Now that he'd listened to Adrienne's platitudes, he valued Genie's candid honesty.

But her honesty had slipped slightly the last time they were together. She'd lied when she'd tried to convince him that she didn't love him.

Or had she been trying to convince herself?

Sweet Genie.

As if all Will had put her through hadn't been enough, he'd ridden into town and into her life looking for revenge. He'd set out to make her love him and succeeded. Despite her words to the contrary, he knew she still loved him. It was there in her eyes.

He'd won.

Or had he?

Why did he miss the sound of her laughter, ache for the feel of her by his side during the night? Of all the women he'd made love to, she was the only one he couldn't seem to put out of his mind.

Why?

The answer hit him like a bolt of lightning. While he'd been busy making Genie fall in love with him, he'd slowly but surely fallen in love with her, too.

What on earth was he going to do about it?

Saturday morning, Genie was walking home from the library when she heard the roar of a motorcycle engine coming up behind her. It came even with her, then stopped.

She was afraid to hope it was Alex. What would he be doing in Wiley this weekend? And why did she want to see him, anyway? Everything had been said between them.

She glanced to the side. When she saw Alex sitting on the powerful black machine, she was tempted to rub her eyes to make sure she wasn't seeing things.

"Hello, Genie. Want a ride home?"

"It's only half a block." As soon as she said it, she was sorry. It was only half a block, but it would have been half a block of physical closeness to Alex.

Before she could tell him she'd changed her mind, he said, "I'll meet you there, then." The bike roared to life again and Alex took off.

By the time she reached home, Alex was standing on her front porch waiting. She stepped past him and opened the door. Standing in the hallway, she stepped back and let him walk past her. Today he was wearing blue jeans and a white sweatshirt that said Yankee Motorworks in red, white and blue letters.

Genie steeled herself to fight back the urge to fall into his arms, but he made no attempt to touch her. Instead he walked into her living room and sat down on the couch.

"Would you like something to drink?"

"Not at the moment, thanks."

Genie started to sit on the love seat, but Alex patted the cushion next to him. She sat, but left enough room between them so they weren't touching.

"You didn't say anything about coming to Wiley this weekend."

"It was a rather impromptu decision." He looked at his hands, which were folded together in his lap. "I wanted to apologize for the way I acted last time I was here."

"I think we both said things we wish we hadn't."

He reached out and tilted her face until she was looking at him.

"Did you mean it when you said you didn't think you really loved me?"

Was he here to extract his final revenge? Well, let him have it. If it would help ease the hurt she'd caused him as a teenager, he was welcome to it. "No, I didn't."

"Then you do love me?"

"Yes, I love you, Alex." *And losing you hurts a hundred times more than losing Will did.*

He moved his hand away from her and stood up. She thought he was going to leave. She bit down hard on her bottom lip to keep from crying out. Instead, he reached into his pocket and pulled out a small velvet box. He sat down, closer to her than before.

Stunned, Genie watched as he slowly opened the box, then turned it toward her. Her breath caught in her throat as the clear white marquise-cut diamond caught a ray of sunlight.

"It's beautiful."

"Would you marry me, Genie?"

She looked at him. "I don't know what to say."

"A yes or no would be fine."

"Are you sure you want to do this?"

"I wouldn't have asked if I wasn't sure."

"But what about all the women, Alex? I glanced through a tabloid someone left in the teacher's lounge and it said the volume of your mail has tripled and that you're receiving propositions and marriage proposals."

"I don't care about those women, Genie. The only one I care about is you."

She wanted so much to believe him. "How can you be sure?"

"They're not interested in *me*. They just want to be able to say they've been with a Yankee hunk. Their stereotyping is just as narrow-minded as the bullies who wouldn't accept me because I had braces and glasses."

"I'm sure not all of them are like that. Maybe you should date a few."

One brow quirked up. "You want me to date other women?"

"Of course not, but I want you to be positive that you won't have any regrets if we do get married."

"Given time, I'm sure all this furor will die down. Rorke, Jesse and I have no plans to follow up the billboard or ads. And I won't go into details, but I've had enough time playing the field to know that what we have between us is special."

She reached out and put her arms around his neck. "What we have together *is* special."

"I thought I could walk away and forget about it, but I can't. I love you, Genie."

"I love you, too."

"Is that a yes, then?"

"Yes."

He pulled her tightly against him and brought his mouth down over hers.

Long, sweet moments later, he straightened. Taking the ring out, he slipped it over her finger, then stretched her arm out in front of them so they could admire it.

Genie turned in his arms and found his lips with hers again. "I love you," she whispered.

"I love you, too. I will always love you."

I will always love you. The words echoed through her mind as he kissed her.

She wasn't sure how, but she ended up flat on her back with Alex leaning over her. He sat up and untwined her arms from his neck.

"Alex?"

"I'm not going anywhere." He ran his hands slowly down the length of her. "I just want to get you out of your shoes."

"My shoes?"

"For starters."

They spent the rest of the morning and early afternoon hours exploring that special magic they wove between them with gentle caresses and less gentle, passion-driven touches.

They started in the living room, but ended up cuddled together in Genie's bed.

The unromantic sound of her stomach grumbling intruded on the moment.

"Hungry?"

"Starving."

"Shall we go out and celebrate?"

"We could fix something in the kitchen and celebrate here."

"Tempting offer, but I want to take you out. So, get up and get dressed."

"Giving orders already?"

He smiled at her. "Please, let's go out to dinner?"

Genie groaned. "That's even worse. You know I can't say no to your dimple."

"Which one?"

Twelve

They took Genie's car, leaving Alex's motorcycle in the garage. Genie gave most of her attention to Alex, but she had recognized the road and knew it led past Roseleigh.

She assumed they were going to have dinner in Calhoun and was surprised when Alex turned into the driveway at Roseleigh. She tried to ask him questions, but he rushed her in and upstairs.

He opened a door and led her into a large bedroom suite. Genie was surprised to see her mother, sister, Esther Dalton and Grandee in the room.

Her mother rushed over to hug her. "Genie, I'm so happy."

Maggie was next in line. "Why didn't you tell me?"

"Tell you what?"

"What a comedian." Maggie laughed. "So, let's see the ring."

Genie held up her hand.

"It's gorgeous," Maggie said. "Not as gorgeous as my soon to be brother-in-law, but close." Maggie moved over to hug Alex, and Grandee and Esther stepped forward to hug Genie.

Genie returned the hugs, then turned to Alex. "What's going on?"

"You said you would marry me."

"Yes, but..."

"Have you changed your mind?"

"No, but..."

"Haven't you always dreamed of being married at Roseleigh?"

"Yes, but..."

Alex kissed her. "Then get ready and I'll see you in the ballroom."

They were getting married?

Today?

Now?

"But..." Alex was out the door before she could ask him any more questions.

Maggie took her arm and led her over to an armoire and opened the doors. Inside were three wedding gowns. "Mine, Mom's and Grandee's," Maggie explained as Genie looked at each dress in turn.

Genie tried on the dresses. They all agreed that Grandee's looked as if it had been made for her.

"I'd be afraid something might happen to it," Genie said.

Grandee put her hand on Genie's shoulder. "Please don't worry about that. It would make me very happy to have you wear it. Alex has always been special to me and it would make me very happy for his bride to wear my dress."

Genie gave in.

Maggie nodded. "Good, if that's settled, then let's get your hair and makeup done."

Genie sat quietly in front of the large mahogany vanity table and let Maggie handle the details. She could hear the voices of the other women in the room, but she wasn't paying attention to what was being said.

Genie's thoughts were racing at warp speed. Alex had said they were going to dinner, and here she sat halfway through being transformed into a bride.

She'd said she would marry him, but they hadn't discussed where they would live and what she would do about her job. Had he assumed she would drop her life and go with him?

She remembered the way he'd roared into town a week before Grandee's birthday party and changed the location. Was she prepared to put all her personal goals on hold for Alex as she had for Will? As her mother had done for her father?

She loved him and wanted to marry him, but...

"I need to see Alex," she said.

"But you're in your wedding gown," her mother said. "It will be bad luck. It's bad enough that you saw him at all today."

What would her mother say if she knew they'd spent the morning and afternoon making love? "I need to talk to Alex."

Grandee walked over to stand next to Genie, placing one hand on her arm. "I think it would be even worse luck for Alex to marry an uncertain bride. Esther, go get the young scamp."

Alex's grandmother left the room. She returned shortly. Alex was with her, looking devastatingly handsome in a black and white tuxedo with a red rose in his lapel.

Genie's first instinct was to run to the comfort of his arms. Instead she looked at Grandee. "Could we talk alone, please?" she asked.

The room emptied until only Genie and Alex were left.

"You wanted to see me?" Alex's voice was tight, his mouth drawn in a grim line.

"Yes."

He stayed where he was, a few steps into the room. "Here I am."

"Alex . . ."

"Listen, if you want to call this off, just say so. Don't try to sugarcoat it and for heaven's sake don't beat around the bush."

She stood and walked across the room to stand in front of him. The stiff slip she was wearing crinkled with each step. "I just want to talk a few things over first . . . this is all happening so fast."

He placed his fists on his hips. "Well?"

"Alex, what about my job? I love teaching. I don't want to give it up."

Some of the tension seemed to drain out of him. "I'm not asking you to. In fact, the week after we get back from our honeymoon, you've got an interview at the Maitland Academy. It's a private elementary school, which my secretary assures me is the best in the area."

"You set up a job interview for me?"

"Yes. I didn't think you would mind."

Besides organizing the wedding, he'd taken the time to look into jobs for her. All those details taken care of before he even knew she would accept his proposal. "I'm stunned. And not sure what to say."

"All I'm asking is that you give the place a chance. Check it out. Check the other options in commuting range, then if you can't find something, I'll start looking into moving Yankee headquarters. But it would take awhile, it's not something I could fix overnight."

"You'd do that for me?"

"Of course. What did you expect?"

"I didn't know what to expect. We'd never discussed it."

"I didn't think we had to. I thought you'd know we were going into this marriage together as partners. We're both going to be making adjustments."

She'd been projecting Will's behavior onto him again. "Alex, it's going to take me a while to get used to being with someone who's so considerate of my feelings. There's such a fine line between compromising and being a doormat, and I'm afraid I got used to doing the second when I was with Will."

"The misunderstanding wouldn't have happened if I'd discussed everything with you. Normally we would discuss something this important beforehand, but I wanted the wedding to be a surprise. I wanted to give you your dream wedding."

He opened his arms.

She went into them.

He kissed her forehead. "All better now?"

"Yes."

"Anything else you want to ask?"

"No."

"Ready for me to send your father in?"

Long-imagined visions of her walking down the aisle toward Will drifted to the front of her mind. "No."

"No?"

"I want *you* to walk down the aisle with me. If you don't mind."

He smiled. "I don't mind at all."

They stepped into the ballroom. Candles lit the room with a warm glow as the last of the sunlight faded away outside. Friends and family filled rows of chairs set before the minister.

Maggie and Grandee stood on one side of Reverend Banks, Rorke and Jesse on the other.

The scent of roses hung in the air. A small chamber orchestra began the wedding march.

"Is it the way you dreamed it would be?"

Genie looked up at Alex. "It's perfect. Thank you."

The day of the parade, when she'd told Alex about the plans for her wedding, he'd remarked that the most important part of a wedding should be who you were marrying. Now she realized how true his words had been.

The ballroom was beautiful and it was nice to have so many friends and family there to share the moment with them, but by far the most important detail was the man by her side.

The man she had pledged her love to . . . the man she was about to pledge her life to.

They reached the front of the room and the ceremony began. The words and the vows were solemn, but the smiles they exchanged were full of happiness and love.

When Reverend Banks told the groom he could kiss his bride, Alex did just that. A kiss full of promise to seal the vows they'd made.

The kiss continued until Genie heard Rorke clear his throat.

With a sigh, Alex moved his mouth off hers. But he didn't let her go. His arms pulled her even closer against him, his head nuzzling against her neck.

"Alex, are you okay?" she asked, loud enough so only he could hear.

He straightened to his full height. Taking her face between his palms, he smiled at her. "I'm fine. But I'm dying to get you out of... your shoes, Mrs. Dalton."

* * * * *